HaLLoWeeN PartY '21

Being a Miscellany to Unequivocally Terrify and Disconcert the Young and Aged

Halloween Party '21

Designed and edited by Dianne Pearce and David Yurkovich.

"The Halloween Hound" was originally published in the October 2020 issue of
Next Page Ink Arts and Literary Magazine.

Other volumes in the **Halloween Party** series:

Halloween Party 2017
Halloween Party 2019

gravelightpress.com

ISBN: 978-1-7340918-4-7
Library of Congress Control Number: 2021943901

Contents

"Horror is the removal of masks."
Robert Bloch

HaLLoWeeN ParTy '21

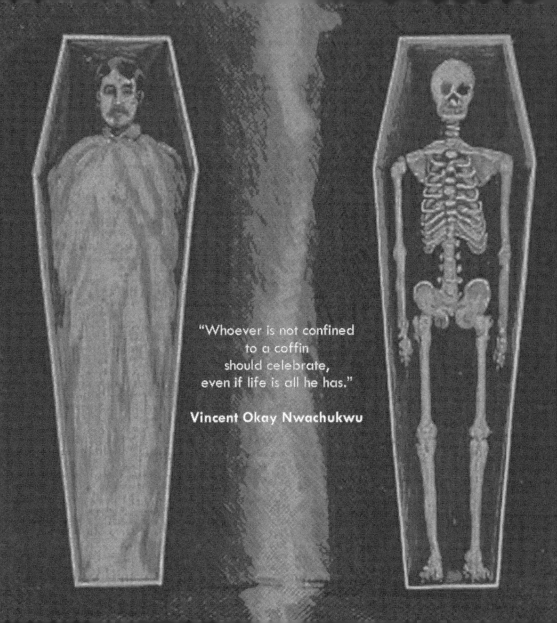

"Whoever is not confined
to a coffin
should celebrate,
even if life is all he has."

Vincent Okay Nwachukwu

Introduction

They say that "dead men tell no tales," but David W. Dutton has just proved them all wrong. And I imagine that, in the beyond, he is chuckling as he reads that. David, in my recollection of him as a member of my local writing group, liked to go about life in his unassuming way and then dazzle and amaze us with his stories.

By now, you may well have figured out that David has died. It was, as I pen this introduction, quite recently, and it is with sadness and love that Dave Yurkovich and I dedicate this book to him.

David was the first person to arrive at my house in 2016 on the day of the inaugural meeting of the Milton Workshop, invitations having been posted in local coffeeshops and on local social media. To show up at a complete stranger's house, especially in an area that was once so small (less than 1,000 residents) that everyone knew everyone else, takes a certain personality type. David had it. He was a mixture of humility, certainty, *joie de vivre*, mischief, and kindness. We shared a love of dogs and children and—I only found out after his passing—deviled eggs (perhaps why we both like horror so much, because the eggs are, you know, deviled).

David kept his friends (among whom Dave and I count ourselves) close and his family closer. I knew him as a man equally in love with his wife at the end of his life as he was when they first met, around his twelfth year on Earth. Doubtless he would have liked a few more years to express his love to her because I think it was his greatest pleasure. David was also a fierce, protective, and loving father and grandfather; everything else could damn well wait if the kids needed him.

I feel so sad and sorry for myself to have lost David. And so lucky to have one last Dutton original to share with everyone.

As a publisher, my mission is to provide talented writers in the second half of their lives a platform in which to reach an audience with their work. I am thankful to have done so for David, and he and I, from the beyond and the here, encourage all who have stories within themselves to "Finish your damn novel!" (short story, poetry collection, or memoir).

In addition to David Dutton's haunting tale, this collection features several folks who are on their way to wonderful careers in writing. You'll find two tales of speculative horror by James Goodridge. A collection of these stories will be prowling for fresh blood in 2023. If you haven't yet encountered James's monstrous detectives, prepare to be scared and hooked. R. David Fulcher is no stranger to horror and is wrapping up a heart-stopping collection for Gravelight arriving in 2022. A word of warning: David's story is not for the claustrophobic or those who fear the dark. Bernie Brown writes clever tales of unnatural retribution. We're proud to showcase two of her delightful and terrible gems, and we're also proud to be the home for her horror collection creeping out from under the bed while we're all asleep in 2023.

Yet another David (my partner in crime, David Yurkovich) brings his unique style of nostalgia horror to us in a tale sure to resonate with anyone unwise enough to stay out too late on Halloween night (you know who you are).

Russell Reece has contributed a poem to the collection. What qualifies a poem as horror? If you're all alone when you scream, does it make a sound? When a poem provides the answer to this second question, you know it has also answered the first. Robert Fleming's poem is also going to elicit a scream, as it perfectly immortalizes one of the most famous scenes in horror fandom.

JC Raye adds a supernatural twist to the ugly brutality of war. When justice comes, it does not arrive kindly. Phil Giunta, a prolific writer adept in multiple genres, tells a story that will warm your heart … and then break it.

We also are thrilled to introduce some new authors to the *Halloween Party* series:

Jeffrey D. Keeten tells a story bound up like a cypress tree in Spanish moss and reveals that sometimes the only way to release tangled things is to cut them free. Nancy North Walker takes us into a future where death is small, and invasive, and ruthless, and mean. Faye Perozich delivers a psychological tale of terror and shows how a broken heart breaks more than itself—you are encouraged to keep yours safe as you read along. Kim DeCicco takes a look at mother-daughter relationships and what we pass, deadly-down, to the next generation. Morgan Golladay offers both poetry and prose on the subject of all things fall and creepy, and her vampire tale will make you rethink any romantic notions of lovers with sharp teeth.

Lastly is a tale that was retold to me, based on local scuttlebutt. If you're in the area on a quiet and creepy moonless night, you may want to take a ride out there to see what you can see. As I like to poke around in none-of-my-business, this tale is the first in a collection of local stories unveiling the haunted past of Sussex County that Gravelight is releasing in the coming months.

Thanks to readers like you, I had the great privilege of bringing David Dutton's stories to the world before he left it. Thank you for helping Dave Y. and I do what we love to do as both writers and publishers. My dear departed David, we love you; we miss you; we hope the afterlife provides you reunion with all the beloved dogs who went before you, good stories to tell for the day when you are reunited with your loved ones, and the opportunity to haunt a little on the side so you can keep giving the world the occasional scare.

Dianne Pearce
Milton, DE
August 2021

"Live your life, do your
work, then take your hat."
Henry David Thoreau

CHIROPTERA LAMIA
Quia sanguinem sitienti

The East 55th Street Affair

James Goodridge

A wind-blown, empty tin can bounces down East 55th Street, past a nondescript house at 1:00 a.m. It makes a sound that stirs visceral suspicion in a large-framed man, a lock of blond hair interfering with his tortoise shell eyeglasses as he strides down a dimly lit hallway to a section of the house facing Broadway Avenue. The man is large. So large, in fact, that he carries another man over a dark-flannel-suited shoulder as if he was little more than an extra sweater.

To the distant observer, it would appear that the man is being carried to safety. Closer inspection, however, would reveal a recent strangulation. A pencil-thin mustache above blue lips matches the iced-blue death stare of his eyes. The poor soul, a lake sailor, is about to have his head detached from his body by sharp-knifed precision. Back in the far end of the house, the laker's dipsomaniac companion lay face down, resting on a kitchen table in a post-18th-Amendment repeal blackout, and will soon meet the same fate.

"Now hold still, sir, and lay here. Not that you could move." The large man chortles as he dumps the victim on a steel mortician's table, a tool of the business that made up the Broadway Avenue side of the house. Crossing the room, then back to the table, the large man has in his hand a huge glimmering knife, the type suited for bloody work in a Chicago slaughterhouse.

"Time to join the club, sir," the large man says. He tugs down the victim's navy-blue turtleneck and places the knife on the man's neck, intent on slicing into the space between the first and second vertebrae.

—

November 1938

Cleveland was in the midst of a powdered sugar donut dusting of snowfall, the flakes dancing around our New York Central's Cleveland Limited as the passenger train slows on approach to the station. I step down from our steel-green Pullman car at Cleveland's Union Terminal and immediately peg a quartet of men in fedora hats and trench coats who are quickly approaching. Detectives, without a doubt.

"Gentlemen, are you looking for us?" I ask, savoring the last puff of an Old Gold before dropping it to the platform and crushing the tip beneath my Oxfords.

"Are you Madison Cavendish and Seneca Sue SunMountain, the PIs from New York?" asks the eldest-looking of the quartet.

"That's us, honey," Sue confesses. She tips the redcap and takes our luggage from him before handing it to the youngest of our new acquaintances.

Judging from the newness of his pithy trench coat, I figure he'd only recently joined the squad. He issues a puzzled look but nonetheless takes our bags by their handles.

"Our boss is waiting for you on the 12th floor of the Hotel Cleveland; follow us, please," the oldest of the troupe says. The men form a circle around us as we leave the misting steam of the train platform for a corridor connecting the terminal to the hotel.

The swank lobby of the hotel is replete with plush chairs, Persian rugs, potted plants, and flowers no doubt glad to be inside away from the cold. The place is anything but a flop house, the décor a matching display of greens, reds, and goldfinch. From behind the front desk, a live broadcast of ballroom music plays on a radio, the volume set low. A three-fingered brush across the nose from one of our escorts alerts the concierge that we're headed up to the 12th floor and are not to be disturbed.

Off the elevator and onto the 12th, we enter the suite following two raps on the white- and gold-leaf-trimmed door. The baby-faced man, light brown hair parted down the middle, wears a dark-brown suit. His hands outstretch to greet us, but he flinches at our touch. Blue eyes visually size us up. We recognize him, of course, as Eliot Ness, the former Chicago Prohibition-era gang-buster who now serves as Cleveland's public safety director.

"Okay, you guys go down to the lobby and grab coffee or something. I want to speak with Mr. Cavendish and Miss SunMountain alone," Ness says. His "Unknowns," as he calls them (the "Untouchables" tag was Chicago's and Chicago's alone) retreat, while Ness leads us to the sitting area of a suite decorated in Art Deco blacks, teals, and ivories. The style is fading from fashion slowly and unsteadily, like the 1930s itself. Helping my Sue out of her black, g-winged-collar fur chinchilla coat reveals that she's wearing what she describes as

19

her "séance dress," laced satin black-magic onyx and violet. She removes a dark beret, and black hair streaked with magenta flows down onto her shoulders. If her image doesn't stun Mr. Ness into viewing us as a mystery, Sue's rose-tinted glasses may do the trick. A three-piece black suit, Homburg hat, bow tie, and St. James tweed overcoat is my "meet Elliot Ness" attire. We take our seats on two club chairs offered to us.

"I want to first off thank you for making the trip to Cleveland, and also please pass my thanks on to Stuart Kirkland at the Office of Special Concerns in New York for directing me to you. I only hope you can deliver. Permit me to rehash our recent phone conversation. For the past few years, a sadistic madman has terrorized Cleveland. Some refer to him as the Mad Butcher of Kingsbury Run; others call him the Torso Killer. Whatever the vile name, the public nightmare he created must end!" Ness is seated on the suite's sofa, leaning forward and rubbing his tense hands; it's apparent that the case has gotten to him in spades. Next to Ness on the sofa is a flat manilla envelope, along with a white envelope, its contents bulging. A cardboard box rests on the coffee table. A strong smell of ink emanates from the box, as though its contents had only been recently printed.

"You'll find mimeographed summaries of twelve cases we feel he's behind; look them over."

"When did he last strike?" Sue asks.

"This August past. Excuse my French, ma'am, but the piece of shit dumped his eleventh and twelfth victims in view of my office in the Central Standard Building. The bastard thought he was being cute." Ness's blue eyes glare full of vengeful anger.

"And his methods?" I ask.

Ness exhales slowly. "He likes to decapitate and then emasculate the victims while they're alive or right after he's strangled them. He sometimes dismembers his female victims straight, no chaser." Ness moves to the window, looking down on the neon lights of the mostly blue-collar city as if the snow will make this case—or affair, as we call them—melt away.

He walks back to the sofa. "Speaking of methods, Kirkland was a bit closed mouth about yours. He did give me a list of people who could vouch for you. Professor E.E. is in Europe and couldn't be reached. Mr. Robeson is in England on a singing recital tour. Is that *the* Paul Robeson? Anyway, I spoke with Sheriff Kilroy Bertrand from Upstate New York. He was as vague as Kirkland, although he affirms you two get the job done 'like a sip of apple jack,' whatever the hell that means." Sue and I smile at our former client (and now friend's) endorsement, remembering the an earlier case, "The Stumpville Affair."

"I don't like to go into details about our ways and means either," I said, "but be assured we will find your degenerate assassin, whomever he may be. And yes, that is *the* Paul Robeson; he was a client back in '36."

"We already know who the suspect is," Ness admits.

"Come again?" my Sue asks. "You know who he is?"

"Name's Francis Sweeny. He was a prominent surgeon until a taste for strong drink slowed down his career. We hauled him into this very suite for questioning for a full week; had to dry him out a few days first. He failed a polygraph test not once, but twice." Ness leans forward and rubs his hands again in agitation.

"And?" Sue and I ask in unison.

"We haven't a direct tie in evidence for Sweeny, whom we, confidentially, refer to as Gaylord Sunheim. He's well connected in Democratic politics. As a member of the Republican party, I'd have been vilified by the press for going on a witch hunt," Ness admits, as we shake our heads in bewilderment. Regardless of our political affiliations—Sue is a New Deal Democrat while I'm a progressive LaGuardia Republican—we would never allow our allegiances to bend our judgment in an affair.

"My hands are tied. But yours, Mr. Cavendish and Miss SunMountain, are not. In a way, I'm glad that you're confidential about your methods. I've exhausted my options. I want Sweeny behind bars. We need to nab him in the act." Ness reaches for the envelopes, then pushes them across the coffee table to us. Inside the white envelope is the first half of our hefty fee.

"You have a unique problem, Mr. Ness, and we provide unique solutions," I say, sounding like a smooth-voiced radio pitchman. Sue places the white envelope in her black leather clutch bag.

"The county sheriff and his boys tried to get ahead of us with an arrest," Ness explains, "but the only result was the man they nabbed on dubious evidence ended up dying in their custody."

Ness retrieves the cardboard box from the coffee table and rises from the sofa. "I should let you two get anchored in. You're registered downstairs as Mr. Carl La Fong and Miss Tessie Garfield. Order anything you two want from room service. Around 9:00 a.m. tomorrow morning, detective Merylo will pick you up for a tour of the crime scenes. Inside this box is a letter I've written to Cleveland's chief coroner, Dr. Gerber, asking his permission for you to view the assorted remains of the victims he still has preserved."

"Why a letter?" my Sue asks.

"Let's just say the doctor and I are not exactly cordial."

After handshakes, which again cause Ness to flinch due to the coldness of my hands in contrast to the overabundance of pulsing warmth from Sue's, Ness heads for the door, overcoat draped on arm and with hat in hand.

"I'll phone your room at 6:00 p.m. tomorrow for a progress report. Sorry

I didn't think to reserve two separate rooms. Are you okay with the setup?"

"Maddy will sleep on the sofa," Sue lies with a snicker.

We make ourselves at home. Unpacking, I change into my red smoking jacket and ochre PJ bottoms, while Sue wears my ochre PJ top, which I long ago concluded I'll never get back. I recline on the suite sofa, enthralled by the viciousness of the killer's work as I read the case summaries. The reports contrast with Sweeny's kindly neighborhood doctor image and the black and white photograph I remove from the manilla envelope. Movement on the teal carpeted floor of a long black telephone cord snaking from the sitting area into the suite's bedroom indicates my Sue is still checking in with New York. A knock on our door denotes the arrival of room service.

"You've been behaving yourself? Purr the truth now," I overhear Sue ask to the meowed maundering reply of our housecat/familiar, Sekhmet, whose meowing every now and then is mixed with a lisped human-sounding, "Yes, ma'am," which she learned to say a while ago. In my mind's eye, I picture the black-on-black image of Sekhmet, her furry tentacles wrapped around the candlestick phone of our friend and fellow occult detective Elsa Cranberry, while Elsa, with British calm, waits to get on the phone to report to us the devilment Sekhmet has gotten into.

"Sue, tell Sekhmet I send my love. And tell Elsa I'll pay for whatever Sekhmet broke or will break, but right now, our food is getting cold, sweet stuff," I explain. For Sue, a few hot dogs minus buns and condiments. My meal consists of hot water for a pot of hyssop tea and a plate of liver and onions with undercooked liver. It was the only palatable option since blood pudding wasn't on the menu. Off the phone now, Sue is cozy and entangled with me on the sofa, noshing and reading. She sits up and issues an enquiring look.

"Maddy, do you think this Doctor Sweeny is human?" Sue asks, staring at the doctor's photo image.

"Don't know, love. He could be possessed by the demons in his own mind, or he could be possessed by some entity like the one Rollo Ahmed helped us track down in '27—the Demon Box of Ebril. For all we know, contrary to Ness' opinion, Sweeny may not be the killer at all. But if he is some type of demon, my dear, you, me, Ness, and the city of Cleveland are in for more murders."

—

Cleveland's weather refuses to be up-tempo during our stay. A gray, moody, overcast sky, along with the coldness of Cleveland's modest (by New York standards) skyline, is punctuated by airborne soot from the area's various industrial production. I'm quite sure this city's melancholy ambiance, mixed with our search for the Torso Killer, could rival London in 1888 when Jack the Ripper prowled that city's gray streets and alleys.

"Careful making ya way down now; there's patches of ice on the ground," Detective Pete Merylo cautions. A pudgy and graying man, Merylo has worked on the case the longest. We take the advice and carefully step our way down Jackass Hill into the barren Kingsbury Run, a watershed area replete with freight and commuter train tracks. Trees and bushes mugged of their leaves by autumn winds add a gloomy touch. Once a haven for hobos and the downtrodden, and before that, a picnic site for the gilded age well-to-dos, today, all that remains are ghost-like memories and trash. I wouldn't be surprised to learn that if we stood in this area long enough, we'd hear the faint, haunted crooning of Trixie Smith's "Freight Train Blues" vaporing through the Run.

"The victims were dumped here?" Sue asks Merylo. She peeks into a clump of bushes before Merylo can show us. I can tell by her expression that Sue senses what she often describes as an *infinity pull* of death, still active after so many years, in the chill air.

"How'd ya know, young lady?" asks an amazed Merylo. "Victims two and three were found here."

"Just a hunch, Merylo," winks my Sue, minus the rose tints. At times I worry for my love. The infinity pull is a nexus to the underworld. It could manifest itself into multiple raging voices and screams reaching out to her with ghastly tales. Failing to block them out could be very bad.

Merylo pointed a thick finger to the left. "Down that way is where Ness had the shanty town burned down. Had the bums rounded up and marched outta there."

He can tell right away by the looks on our faces that Ness hadn't mentioned that desperate act to us. I figure it was the reason the city newspapers soured on Ness, too. The rest of the crime scene tour, alas, produces nothing.

Merylo chauffeurs us to the coroner's office on Cedar Avenue, a two-story building that also houses the Cleveland Department of Health.

"I'll be out here waiting for ya," he says to Sue and me. "That doctor rubs me the wrong way, and we've had too many clashes through the years over this case. Sammy Gerber listens to too many junior G-man radio shows. Wants to solve cases from his office chair!"

Merylo steps out of the sedan and opens our door. He's nothing if not polite.

"Come pick us up in an hour, Merylo," I say, to which he yells something about lunch before returning to the driver's seat and speeding away.

We're soon inside the reception area of a very clean and antiseptic powder-blue-painted first floor. Sue and I are growing irritated as Doctor Samuel

Gerber stands before us in a white lab coat. He's already read Ness's letter twice and begins reading it a third time, just for spite, as we stand in silence. Gerber adjusts his thick glasses and runs a hand through his receding black hair.

"Ness had no right to send you two here to me," he says. "I told him before, I answer to the citizens of Cleveland, not him. He can contact the mayor with this request. That's the protocol. Anyway, who are you? Doesn't matter. Have Ness contact the mayor and then come back tomorrow."

"Doctor Gerber, we're kind of pressed for time," Sue explains.

"It can wait until tomorrow," Gerber replies, handing back the letter. He turns to walk away, but I jump in front of him and block his path.

"Young man, what in Sam Hill are you doing? Get ... get away from me, I say!"

"Doctor Gerber, look at me," I order, removing my green-tinted glasses. I make eye contact and immediately gain control of his mind. Soothing him at first with a mental flashback to his childhood self, dressed in knicker pants and reading *Tom Swift and the Visitor from Planet X* on his parents' front porch, I then project an image of what will befall him should he refuse to accommodate us. The doctor quietly gasps in terror.

"I ... I apologize. What can I ... do for you?" Gerber stammers.

"Show us the body parts from the Torso Killer case, Doctor," I insist, retaining eye contact.

He walks slowly to the receptionist's desk. "Miss Herrington, call down to the basement. Tell Vernon ... I'm sending two people down ... to examine the physical remains related to the Kingbury Run case. They're not to be ... interrupted ... in any way. Also, tell Vernon he can go to lunch."

Lula Mae Herrington, a mahogany-complexioned plump woman in a flowery print dress covered by a rust-colored sweater, barely glances up from her

26

desk. She looks uneasy as she picks up the receiver but simply nods and replies, "Yes, Doctor Gerber."

We step away from Herrington. I turn to Gerber and whisper, "Doctor, you will go upstairs to your office, sit calmly behind your desk, take the phone off its hook, and wait for me."

Gerber quietly ascends the stairs while Sue and I begin our trek into the basement morgue room.

—

"Right this way," Morgue Assistant Vernon Quincy, a tall, lean man of fair hair and gray temples, says. Vernon opens a dark wood cabin then gingerly removes a large glass jar. The smell of tissue fixative and embalming formaldehyde sweeps across the morgue room to engage. It's equally as bad as Vernon's lunch, a wax paper-wrapped egg salad sandwich resting on a nearby stone slab sink counter. He retrieves a wooden box and places it on the same counter. "I guess you can start with victims four and eight. I'll be back after lunch if you need to look at more. If not, just leave the evidence on the counter. But be careful; I don't want Doc Gerber to be sore with me if something happens." Vernon removes his lab coat and hangs it on a hook near the doorway. He then opens a body locker and pulls out a cold bottle of milk, grabs his sandwich, and heads out.

We get to work.

The jar before Sue contains a male human head. A tag affixed to the lid reads *Tattoo man No. 4, E. 55th St.* The victim appears to have been in his late twenties. My Sue unscrews the lid and immerses her hands into the jar. She tilts the victim's head at an angle so that their eyes meet. The dead man's eyelids flutter open. Whispering, Sue begins to converse with him.

I open the top of the wooden box labeled *Rose. W, No. 8 Lorain-Carnegie Bridge.* To one side is a dried blood-encrusted burlap bag; the other side contains a collection of bones: ribs, humeri, ulnas, radii, and femurs. I bite my fingertips, drawing magenta-speckled blood. I touch the haversack and several bones, and a tortured voice enters my mind.

"I'm Rose. It's a sweltering liquored-up blues song warbling summer night. I leave a roaring Third Ward bar with a large ofay man who says he's got the hots for a little brown gal like me. He wants to take me to his home and love me for a price. I don't believe the love spiel, but what the hell? It's the good time that counts. He places a hand around my waist as we walk towards East 55th Street. He points to his house in the distance. The closer we get, the tighter his grip becomes. 'Ease up, love,' I say, 'ease up.' He leads me inside the house and locks the door. His hands surround my neck like a vise. I try to wrest free but ... Jesus ... I can't breathe! My body grows more limp by the second. Oh Lord ... I ..."

I pull my fingertips away. Rose's life, no matter how hard a road she'd traveled, was important and didn't deserve the fate handed her. She mattered. And although we don't look it, Sue and I are of mixed race. (It's an open secret in Harlem.) This kinship of ethnicity we share with Rose fills me with an added incentive. We must stop the maniacal doctor.

Back in the here and now, I look over at Sue, who's ended her conversation with tattoo man, tears streaming down her freckled cheeks. We embrace each other to steady and compose ourselves. Sue tells me that even in death, tattoo man wouldn't reveal his identity as he wished to spare his family from the emotional turmoil he believed they'd suffer should they learn about his life's actions.

—

Merylo returns to pick us up.

"So, ladies and gentlemen, how'd ya make out?" he asks, looking down at the bandages (given to me by Lula Mae) on my fingertips.

"Swell, Merylo. Just swell," I answer, more than a little fatigued.

"How about a few Polish boys?" he offers.

"What?" I ask.

"Excuse me?" demands Sue.

"Ha ha! The best of Cleveland." Merylo explains that a "Polish boy" is a hot dog with everything, including fried potatoes. Having been through our latest ordeal, I welcome an activity as benign as eating a hot dog.

"Sounds exquisite," I say. "But first, a short detour at the nearest thrift shop if you don't mind."

"Maddy!" Sue screams, as the three of us set in the flivver just as Merylo is about to pull onto the road. "You forgot about Dr. Gerber!"

"Shit!" I exclaim, darting from the auto and running back into the building to restore the doctor's free will.

—

Two days later, around 1:00 a.m., my blood, along with whatever the lifeforce of a horror from beyond the stars lurks within me, rushes to my head. Sweeny is carrying me, my body folded over his left shoulder, down a dim hallway. Destination unknown. Sue is in the kitchen, face down on the table, feigning unconsciousness from excessive alcohol consumption.

The good doctor thought he had strangled the piss out of me. We enter another room. The same scent from the department of health enters my nostrils. I'm dropped onto a cool steel table. Motionless, I look up at Sweeny and issue a blue-eyed, dead carp stare.

"Now hold still, sir, and lie here. Not that you could move." Big man laughs at his own pun. "So nice of you and your female friend to have accompanied me to my home. But now it's time for you to join the club, sir," Sweeny says, placing a knife, just the right size to gut a steer, to my neck. Just then, I hear Sue scream from the kitchen as she begins to rise in willing surrender to the full moon's glow from a nearby window. The start of her Lycan transformation has begun. I also rise.

Sweeny turns, distracted by Sue's scream. I use the opportunity to grab the knife from Sweeny and swing my legs off the table. The doctor backs away but then advances, his face blushing with rage. The sound of dress fabric being torn apart can be heard in the kitchen.

"Listen, old man, you're not in a good position," I explain. Then, to prove my point, I tighten the grip on the knife with my right hand and thrust its blade into the palm of my left. After a moment's pause, I withdraw the knife, snap the blade in two, and toss it to Sweeny. He backs into a corner of the room, knocking over a metal stand and a tray containing shiny surgical tools of the undertaker trade.

"Nasty people," Sweeny says, voice cool as frost. "Have to understand I'm not well. Family, fellow doctors, they all have tried to help. But not enough help to get me away from these nasty people around me. Nasty people. I was the only one to do good among my brothers, but nobody cared. Look at you, you Great Lakes bum, you're one of those nasty people, too. You and that drunken mutt you brought along. What do you think you're going to do? Take me in? Nasty people. Schoolboy Ness couldn't prove crap. I'll plead insanity. And that little knife trick won't stop me from ripping your nasty head off."

Sweeny babbles on, and it's clear he'll keep babbling on, so I step to him and issue a good-old left hook to the face. His glasses fly across the room. I lift him off his feet and hold him up by his murderous neck. Sweeny manages to bellow out a baritone scream as I bare my fangs.

Claws scratch at the door Sweeny had closed to perform sick work.

"Excuse me, old man," I say.

With Sweeny dangling and struggling in midair, I unlock the door. My sempiternal love growls, lumbered in wolfish silver-gray fur with a magenta streak running down her back. Sue, now twice her body size, surprises me. Typically she would have bashed the door into pieces. My Sue and I gaze into each other's eyes, knowing we can't let Sweeny go on. I drop him and then jump down beside him as he lies whimpering on the floor.

"I'll see you nasty people in Hell!" snivels Sweeny.

"I wouldn't be surprised if you do, old man. You see, in the course of our business, we do travel to that troffy part of town from time to time to drop mugs like you off in person. Either way, the commissions are good." Sue growls a giggle.

I bite into Sweeny's neck. His warm alcohol-laced blood flows down my throat like a just-uncorked bottle of vintage Moët. I make room at his bloody trough for Sue to gnaw on his throat. She wastes little time in chewing up pieces of flesh, flipping the choice bloody bits in the air, and then snapping them into her maw. The man who had terrorized Cleveland for over five years is finished at last.

After our repast of the doctor, we clean up and discard our thrift store wardrobe. Suitcases with a change of clothes, which Sweeny thought to be the sad belongings of two vagabonds, await us in the kitchen. There are also two bottles of Schenley's Golden Wedding Rye—one full, one empty—bait Sweeny used in his effort to lure us in.

Now we face the dilemma of getting rid of Sweeny's body since we'd

gone against Ness's arrest order. Or have we? I gaze at the instruments the
doctor knocked and formulate an idea.

—

The following afternoon is sunny as we pack our bags in anticipation of
the evening Limited back to the Big Apple. Ness meets us at our hotel, and we
bring him up to speed on recent events.

"Sweeny was able to get away with his crimes by renting out his house
of horrors from an absentee undertaker landlord strapped for money," I explain.
"When he wasn't luring victims from taverns to his home, Sweeny made money
'no questions asked' by working as a mob fix-up doctor, treating gunshot
wounds and the like for the underworld."

"Maddy and I figured Sweeny would venture onto new hunting
grounds," Sue continued, charming as always. "His old pick-up place, the
Buckeye Inn, had become too hot. Too many of the victims had a common roost
there. We decided to lure him to us by masquerading as the type of victims he
coveted. Enter Carl La Fong, an unemployed Great Lakes merchant marine, aka
Madison, and his hard-drinking shrewish girlfriend, Tessie Garfield, aka yours
truly. We settled on a place on East 9th Street, a bar named Nap's Tap Room. It
was Sweeny's type of watering hole, and we provided the silage to satisfy his lust
for bloodshed."

Ness sits uneasily on the sofa. The white envelope next to him contains
the second half of our fee. In the corner of the room, a white linen-covered
serving cart holds the remains of our breakfast—plates of meat pies, well-spiced
in a rich sanguine gravy, along with the blood pudding I so often crave. I had
slipped the kitchen staff a Ben Franklin for use of the space that I might perform

some pre-dawn culinary magic.

"But, what about Sweeny? What happened to him?" Ness asks, leaning forward impatiently.

"Forgive me, old man, but you really didn't want us to nab Sweeny, did you?" I ask.

He pauses long enough to conceive and bring a child into the world. "For the greater good," Ness finally replies, "the doctor had to be finished." Ness pauses again, and I suspect he finds it ironic that he sounds as if he's confessing. "We just couldn't have him on the streets. You know that. But again, what did you do with him? I can't have any loose ends."

"It's all been handled," I explain. "Let me give you some veridical advice, Ness: let it go, old man."

Sue and I issue a stoic glimpse over to the room service cart of heavily spiced leftovers. Ness, being the sharp-as-nails lawman that he is, follows our glimpse to the cart and catches the scent of the unusual aroma. A look of horror and nauseousness crashes onto his face.

"Excuse me," Ness manages, and flees to the bathroom to retch.

Later, before leaving Cleveland, we settle accounts with a peaked-looking Ness who is still visibly shaken.

Ness had a long history of dealing with the underworld. What he hadn't counted on was running into Sue and yours truly from another type of underworld.

"Darkness is but a door,
scary Not because It OpeNs,
but out of fear that
It wILL never close."

JoNathaN JeNa

Aristotle's Lantern

R. David Fulcher

They were moving on without him, their head lamps bobbing off in the darkness. Tom, last in the caving group, lagged more and more behind. They never noticed he was no longer there. He didn't mind, though. Finally, he would be alone to photograph the unusual rock formations without the group leader constantly urging him onward through the cave.

He found his way into a small chamber. Over thousands of years, mineral deposits caused the stalactites hanging from the ceiling to join with the stalagmites rising from the floor, creating odd-shaped column structures.

The bright light from his headlamp illuminated two passages from this room—one leading back to the main passage and one off to the corner. The tunnel in the corner was small, about the width of the average plumber, and he would have to wriggle his way through. For a moment, Tom contemplated the wisdom of going off on his own. He weighed the dangers of the cave versus the excitement of exploration. He made up his mind. *No guts, no glory,* he thought to himself. Besides, he could always catch up with the group later if his choice of paths proved to be a dead end.

He stepped over a rock ledge to the entrance of the small passage and crouched down to let the lamp on his helmet light the tunnel. Although a tight fit, it could still be navigated by crawling on his belly and pushing his backpack in front of him.

He wriggled into the tunnel. While his caver's suit protected him from the mud and rock, it did little to alleviate the psychological impact of the tight, dark place. Tom felt as if the entire weight of the mountain was pressing down on him as he pushed himself forward, but he was determined to fight the claustrophobia and continue.

After moving slowly for what seemed like an unbearable distance, the passage released him and opened into a large chamber. Tom was sweating quite a bit, but he was also able to stand up in the large room and stretch his sore muscles.

Panning his light around the chamber, Tom was impressed by his discovery. The room was dominated by a shallow pool so smooth and clear that the entire ceiling reflected on its still surface as a mirror image. Unfortunately, Tom's hopes of going on further were dashed as the opposite wall held only a stone curtain, called so because though it resembled flowing folds of fabric rather than rock, it was impenetrable.

He couldn't go forward, but he was still very excited. This photo of the perfect mirror of the cave would be the stuff of dreams. He rummaged through his pack for his camera and flash assembly.

Tom was attaching the flash to the camera when he was jolted by a sound as if the water in the pool made a slosh and a splash. As he turned the light toward the pool, he was astonished to see that the water's smooth glass skin had been disturbed. Silent currents raced just beneath the surface. Slowly putting his gear aside, Tom cautiously moved to the water's edge for a better look.

While some water was indeed splashing against the sides of the pool, the greatest displacement of water was further out in the pool. A whirlpool was forming as if a giant drain plug had suddenly been yanked out of the bottom. The bare stone sides of the basin were exposed by the water rapidly draining away.

Tom was perplexed, but realizing this was a fleeting opportunity, he quickly reached for his camera. He fumbled with the flash while he watched the pool. Finally, the light clicked into place, and he took aim. He quickly snapped off some shots of the draining pool and the curtain formation, regretting not being quick enough to capture the pool in its pristine condition.

It was then, after satisfying his artistic needs, that he began to worry. Clearly, whatever he'd witnessed was an uncommon geological event. Perhaps there'd been a minor shift in the earth's crust, and it was just his luck to be underground when it happened. While he had heard his fair share of stories from more experienced cavers, none of them included mysterious whirlpools. Whether the emptying of the pool and the shift of the earth's crust was good or bad luck remained to be seen. Then, of course, there was the fact that he had foolishly set off on his own, and the group had no idea of his whereabouts.

Whatever the cause, if this dead-end chamber was becoming unstable, it would be prudent to leave immediately but, overtaken by curiosity more than dread, Tom did not leave. Instead, he stood there staring, camera in hand, as the pool gradually lowered.

An opening became visible at the pool's base as expected, but there was more. To Tom's amazement and horror, something squirmed to get out of the opening, fighting clumsily against the drag of the draining water.

Its features were indistinct in the darkness and, at first, to Tom, it appeared to be all mouth and no body. Finally, it wrestled itself out of the hole, and then out of the pool, and onto the muddy ground. Focusing his lamp on it, Tom thought, *Is that ... an armadillo? No.* It had no eyes that Tom could see, but nonetheless, it slowly turned its body in his direction and then lunged toward him.

Reason overcame Tom's sudden shock, and he knew he had to get out of there. Steadying himself for a final photo, he took a picture of the thing, and in the temporary blindness from the flash, he had the terrible thought that it was somehow right beside him.

His sight came quickly back to him, and Tom was grateful to see that the creature had made little progress in his direction.

He chanced one more look back while throwing his camera in his pack. Confident that the creature had not quickened its approach, Tom wriggled back into the passageway.

The tunnel seemed more oppressive than before, and Tom's breath labored as he pushed the pack forward and belly-crawled along. He paused once and swore he heard a grating sound that must be the creature following at a glacial pace behind him.

Suddenly his pack wedged up against something as he tried to push it forward. He shoved hard, using both arms, but the pack barely moved. *Had there been a cave-in?* Tom was overcome with fear. If the passage was blocked, he would have to turn around, back toward the dead-end room ... and the creature.

Before Tom could consider his next move, he felt his pack being wrenched from his hands! In the dim light of the lamp, he watched wide-eyed as his pack was violently shaken side-to-side against the walls of the passage. The clattering of the pack's contents was so deafening in the tunnel's silence that

Tom wanted to cover his ears or scream.

Just as quickly, the thrashing stopped, and something began to squirm over the pack. Something with a gaping mouth ringed with five large razor-sharp teeth. Tom screamed and thrust his body backward, leaving the pack behind. *How has the thing I left in the chamber gotten ahead of me?*

As he scrambled backward, Tom's right boot kicked something. He tested the space warily again with his boot, and it was still there. Then it began to move, climbing over his boot.

Tom screamed again and looked back toward the way he had come in. The second creature was still there and continued its deliberate advance over his pack and toward him. Tom began to whimper, and in the silence, it was deafening, so he covered his ears.

"There is something haunting in the light of the moon."
Joseph Conrad

Insecticide

Nancy North Walker

Her laptop dinged. A still shot from a video floated under the date on Screen3, Tuesday, June 22, 2032. A woman in the distance was seated in her underwear at a vanity. Liz held her breath, tapped *play message*.

A half-foot-high, 3D video popped from the screen. As the camera drew closer to the woman's back, her lower lip quivered. It was *her* mole just below the right shoulder, *her* wild, sandy-blonde hair in a purple scrunchie, *her* light-pink bikini underwear. Then, as if a ghost had been filming her earlier that morning, the camera swung to the top of her oval mirror and zoomed in on her hazel eyes as she had applied mascara. Neon-green text crossed the bottom of the screen: *I like you better in brown mascara than black.* She cringed. More text followed. *I like you better naked.* Three long-lashed emoji eyes winked at her.

She jolted to her feet, and her Café Americana went flying. Brown liquid splattered all over her desk, her laptop, her dress, the floor. Coffee streaks ran down her frozen 3D face on Screen3 like blood. She checked the area code on the message and flinched. Pocatello, Idaho.

Disturbed and embarrassed, Liz slinked down the hall to the ladies' room of the Washington trade association where she worked. Her hands shook as she dabbed dark splotches from her dress. In the mirror, she saw the same wild, dilated eyes she'd seen in her vanity mirror Sunday morning. Her first mysterious message had come from a Santa Fe area code.

That ding had jarred her awake around 7:30 a.m. She'd cracked open an eye, checked the time on her smart-tile, groaned, and rolled over. It had been another late night with her yoga girlfriends at Psychotronic, a trendy Washington hotspot. She'd forgotten to draw her window shade or mute her tile. Again.

When she'd opened that message a few minutes later, she'd gasped. A close-up of her sleeping filled the screen. Same blue tank top. Same lilac sheets. Same necklace she'd forgotten to remove before going to bed. Neon-green text at the bottom had made her bolt upright. *Good Morning, Sunshine! Would love to snuggle you!* She'd shivered, then craned her neck toward the doorway, worried someone might be lurking in the shadows.

She'd tiptoed through the apartment, but no one had jumped at her. Convinced there was a hidden camera in her bedroom, she'd spent the next hour tearing it apart. The only thing she'd found was a few flies and spiders. Then she'd remembered the kids from her building who were always spying on people. Their obnoxious drones had hovered outside her bedroom window more than once. *Mystery solved,* she'd thought.

But the mystery hadn't been solved. Gazing at her enlarged pupils in the ladies' room mirror, Liz faced the ugly truth. Someone was stalking her. From inside her apartment.

———

Detective Megan Conover was forty-something, with a turned-up nose and a take-charge attitude. Her roving green eyes didn't miss a thing in Liz's apartment. She asked to see the stalker's messages. Her brows furrowed. She asked Liz to forward them.

"We get lots more stalking complaints these days. Mostly from women like you who use dating apps." She flashed a wry smile. "Nothing against dating apps. That's how I met my husband."

"Why's there more stalking?"

"Because there's so many stalker toys on the market."

"Stalker toys?"

"Miniature robots that look like houseflies and spiders. They buy them on the deep web."

A shiver ran up Liz's spine. She'd seen plenty of insects when she tore her bedroom apart.

"How do they operate them?"

"Remotely, through an app, usually on a disposable smart-tile. These bots have sophisticated cameras and look and move like real insects. Can squeeze under doors and windowsills."

"Is it safe to stay in my apartment?" Her voice hitched. She hoped the detective didn't notice.

"You should be okay tonight. Most stalkers are harmless. I'll have a security firm sweep your apartment for electronic devices first thing tomorrow. Let's see what they find."

Liz tossed and turned all night. She wondered if some creep was watching her from behind insect camera-eyes or slipping more bots under her front door.

When she answered the door the next morning, she was surprised to see three men in hazmat gear with long metal wands. She asked why they needed

43

extra protection. They said it was precautionary. Sometimes they found a spy-bot with poison in it.

Poison? She felt dizzy, sat at her kitchen table, and stared into space. The team moved methodically through her apartment, wands clicking. If they found a micro-bot that contained poison, that would mean someone was trying to kill her. She couldn't imagine who would want to kill her. Her right leg jittered as it did whenever she was nervous. She'd acquired that tic when she was seven, after outrunning a would-be kidnapper.

When the crew finished, she took a taxi to the office and had an unproductive day. She glanced at her tile every few minutes, anxious for the sweep results. Spent most of her time looking up men she'd met through dating apps, staring at their faces, wondering which of them would want to torment her and why, wondering if unseemly photos of her were floating around the internet. The thought made her queasy. Finally, her tile buzzed. It was Detective Conover.

"They found no hidden cameras or microphones. No poison residues. But they did find trace chemicals from a micro-battery."

Her voice hitched. "What does that mean?"

"You might have had some insect bots in your apartment that the stalker removed before the sweep."

"So, he'll just move them back in?"

"Probably not. Most stalkers move on to the next victim once the police are involved."

"So, what do I do now?"

"Sit tight for a little while. Let's see what happens."

Liz paused. Her chest tightened. "Is he in the area?"

"Hard to say. Lately, half my victims' stalkers are scattered across the country."

"Should I change my phone number?"

"That's your decision. The stalker's messages are very helpful to the investigation."

Conover told Liz to phone or message her immediately if anything else happened. She also asked her to assemble a list of men she'd dated in the past year, starting with the ones who'd been inside her apartment.

Liz had always prided herself on being chill, but now she was a basket case. She'd chewed her nails down to the nubs, and her right leg jittered all day long. Three or four times a night, she'd imagine something crawling on her leg, bolt upright, turn on a light, throw back her covers, and inspect every inch of her bed, including underneath it.

When Detective Conover called a few days later, Liz confessed she was a nervous wreck. The detective recommended she purchase a Bug Stunner, a new hypersonic device that paralyzed insects within a five-cubic-foot radius. Conover said the buzz on police forums was it also disabled insect bots. Liz ordered one and it came the next day. She put the long, black, carbon-fiber cylinder on her nightstand. Stiff bugs littered the floor near her bed the next several days. None of them looked manmade, but she flushed them down the toilet just in case. She slept better knowing the stunner was there.

—

It was a little before eight on a sticky July Sunday when Liz returned from the Sweet Talk Café with a latte and a super-sized blueberry muffin. More than two weeks had passed since the stalker had sent the disturbing video. There'd been nothing since. She was beginning to think he'd moved on and felt more at ease in her apartment.

She planned to work all day at home, making final revisions to an important speech she was drafting for the association president. It was her first plum assignment, and she wanted it to be perfect. Liz pulled her laptop from her tote bag, sat down at her dining table, opened her latest draft on Screen1, savored her first bite of muffin, and plunged into editing. Moments later, she tapped Screen2 to find a better word in her thesaurus app. A message notification dinged and floated across the screen with what appeared to be a screenshot of some copy. She tapped it open and found precisely the same copy that was on Screen1, except the word she'd wanted to replace was highlighted in yellow. The hair stood up on the back of her neck when she read the flashing neon-green text at the bottom: *I think "barrage" might be the word you're looking for.*

Liz yanked Screen2 from its socket, shook it with both hands, and yelled at it as if the stalker was inside, "Whoever you are, LEAVE ME ALONE!" Then she threw it at her sofa. It bounced and landed on the rug with a thud. She retrieved it and walked the perimeter of her living room and kitchen, scanning the ceiling, walls, and floor for insects. "Where's your spy toy, creep? If I find it, I'm flushing it down the toilet."

She returned to the table, plopped Screen2 back into its socket, and started to message Conover. Another ding interrupted her. This time, a hologram of a toilet burst from Screen2, flushing sounds and all. The toilet faded in the background, replaced by a neon green message with 3D insects crawling all over it. "Go right ahead. I have LOTS of toys."

Her skin prickled, and her eyes roamed the walls and ceiling. Was there a fleet of insect bots in her apartment, waiting to be activated? One by one? In swarms?

Stay calm. Make him show you his bot, she thought, marking her message to Conover urgent and pressing send. Minutes passed. She tried to focus on her speech. Then, from the corner of her eye, she saw a fly on top of her muffin. The instant she raised her hand to shoo it, it flew away. *Too quick to be manmade,* she thought. Seconds later, another ding pierced the quiet. She opened it, hoping it was the detective. Instead, a photo of her scowling face filled Screen2. A furry black paw and golden muffin top were in the foreground. She winced. A creepy string of smiley-fly emojis pulled flashing neon-green copy across the screen: *Smile, Liz! You're on candid camera!*

Liz's fear erupted into rage. She stood, pounded her fist on the table, and roared. "Get out of my life, you bastard!" The laptop screens and keyboard bounced. Then she remembered the Bug Stunner, sprinted to her bedroom, and returned, waving it across the walls.

A ding in her pocket startled her. Desperate to hear from Conover, she opened the message. A three-foot hologram of a vampire fly exploded in her face, blood dripping from its teeth. She jerked backward, fell on her butt. Caution-yellow skull-and-bone emojis floated around the fly. Neon-green text flashed. *Pick your poison, Liz!* She covered her head with her hands. Was he going to poison her?

Seconds later, she heard another ding. This time it was Conover. "On my way with sweep team."

Liz replied, "Hurry."

She felt woozy as she stumbled back to her laptop, put the stunner on the floor beside her. Screen 2 dinged again, and she tapped *open*. A cartoon fly turned a large "Be Back Soon" sign on a door, blew her a kiss, and flew off screen. *Psychotic asshole,* she thought.

Then she sensed it. On the wall behind her, up high, just beyond the stunner's current range. A voice inside her head said, "Do it." She spun to her feet and pointed the black cylinder high on the wall. An electronic chirp pierced the silence. Her jaw fell open as the robo-fly tumbled to the floor, landed on its back. Periodic chirps continued as it struggled to flip over. Liz grabbed a glass of water from the table, dumped it on the fly, turned the glass upside down, and imprisoned it. The fly stopped moving.

Liz got down on her belly to look. Lifelike was an understatement. Except for a sliver of silicon peeking from its underside, she never would have guessed it was manmade. She prayed the stalker wasn't nearby. She'd just upped the ante.

Conover and the team arrived a moment later. Her index finger trembled as she pointed at upside-down glass. The sweep chief flashed a smile. "Impressive." He picked up the motionless fly with his tweezers and held it to the light. "Definitely a robo-fly. Second-generation xenobot from the late twenties. No poison reservoir, far as I can tell."

"What's a xenobot?"

"A robot made of biological material. They're working on the fifth generation now." He put the specimen in a jar, wrote a case number on it, and told Conover he'd deliver it to the FBI for analysis. He said they needed to do another full sweep of the apartment.

The detective suggested she and Liz go for coffee someplace quiet while the crew did the sweep. They found an empty corner at the Sweet Talk Café.

"You're my first victim to destroy an insect bot."

"Really?" Liz's half-smile faded to a frown. "Does that mean I'm in more danger?"

"Possibly. But he'll probably go underground. You've given the FBI a valuable piece of evidence."

The detective asked Liz to show her the messages from that morning and grimaced as she scrolled through them. "Lotta venom in that snake."

Liz's jittery right leg shook the tiny café table. Their coffees sloshed. "I can't stay in my apartment. I'm worried he'll slip swarms of insect bots under my door or wait for me in the elevator."

"I can move you to a safe apartment with 24-hour security guards."

"You do that for people?"

"Yes. When they're in danger."

"So, I'm in danger?"

"Quite possibly."

"Oh, dear." She looked down, took a deep breath. "Let's do it."

Conover pulled her phone from her pocket, made arrangements on the spot, then asked Liz if she'd finished the list of men she'd dated in the past year. Liz nodded.

"We're especially interested in anyone who may have had access to academic or military robotics research labs or someone who did research on insects."

A face popped into Liz's head. She'd forgotten about him. How could she forget those prying eyes? "There was this entomologist who worked on government research projects." Liz scrolled through her list, found the man's photo and profile, and showed it to Conover.

"Hmm. Please forward that. Was he ever inside your apartment?"

"Yes. Picked me up at my place. Arrived fifteen minutes early. Sat on the sofa while I finished my makeup."

"So why did you decline a second date?"

"Too shy. Seemed lonely." She paused, looked out the café window. "But mostly, it was because I felt like he was undressing me with his eyes."

"We'll see if he turns up in the FBI's database."

—

Although Liz felt safer in the high-security apartment, the stalker encounters had left her emotionally hobbled. Recurring nightmares disturbed her sleep. In one, a housefly in an elevator transformed into a six-foot vampire fly, pinned her against the wall, and sank its daggered teeth into her neck. In the other, the kiss-blowing fly morphed into a scorpion, jumped from her laptop, and stung her. She woke up most nights soaked with sweat, disoriented, heart pounding.

Almost overnight, carefree, party-girl Liz had vanished, and high-strung-homebody Liz took her place. She was skittish everywhere except her high-security apartment and the office. Walked briskly to and from work, afraid the stalker would leap from an alleyway. Thought every insect was a poison-armed bot. Startled when a message notification dinged on anybody's phone.

She retreated inward, saw almost no one outside of work. She quit her studio yoga classes, did them virtually. Ordered delivery from the Valiant Vegan most nights. Turned down dates with guys she used to see. Gave up nights out with the yoga girls. Every time she looked in the mirror, a frightened woman with scrunched shoulders and lined forehead looked back at her. She wondered if laughing Liz with the wide toothy grin would ever be back.

The void in her social life was filled by an insatiable obsession with stalkers and their toys. When she wasn't at work, she was doing research on her laptop. She often forgot to eat dinner. Devoured technical articles on micro-bots and data on modern-day stalkers instead. She hadn't read engineering articles since she graduated—barely—with an engineering degree in robotics. Party-college-girl Liz had despised them. Now they captivated her. The statistics on stalkers, however, made her skin crawl. The consensus was clear. There were more stalkers than ever, and killer-stalkers were on the rise.

Liz's older sister, Sam, a clinical psychology professor at Berkeley, said she had PTSD, needed counseling and medication. Liz resisted the idea of talking to anyone but Sam, so they live-streamed three nights a week. One evening, Sam offered to introduce Liz to her friend, Woo, who headed the micro-robotics program at the university. Sam said Woo could demystify insect bots for Liz. She said she'd like to meet him.

A few days later, Woo live-streamed her from his lab office. He was fifty-something, had thick rimless glasses and a gray-streaked man-bun.

"It breaks my heart that you're being stalked with something I helped invent."

"You invented insect bots?"

"Ours was among several labs that worked on new ways to help the military find captured soldiers, rescue people trapped in explosions, and locate terrorists."

"Tech's always a double-edged sword."

"I'm amazed you caught your stalker's robo-fly. Tell me how you did it."

Liz told him the story. He said drowning the robo-fly was "brilliant." Said water, oil, thick creams, and gels rendered them inoperable.

Woo pulled an array of insect bots from a drawer: flies, spiders, ticks. Took them apart, showed her what they were made of. Then he removed a fly's chip, loaded it into what looked like a USB flash drive, and stuck it into his laptop. He turned his screens around, showed Liz the bot's operating system. She fired off a barrage of questions. Was there a way to identify where the operator was located? Take control of the bot's operations? Set a timer to activate a bot? The answer to all of them was yes.

—

It was late Sunday evening, and Liz was propped against her bed pillows, completely absorbed in one of the operating manuals Woo had sent. She knew it was getting late and reached for her tile to check the time. A message notification floated across the sound-muted screen. When she opened it, she saw a close-up photo of human skin with pores, hair follicles, and a speck of black in the foreground. Neon-green text said: *Know that song "I've Got You Under My Skin?" You've got me under yours.* She screamed, bounded from her bed, rubbing her hands hysterically all over her skin, then grabbed the stunner, ran it over every inch of her body. A tiny black object dropped to the floor. It was a deer tick, on its back, chirping. Woo's words echoed in her head. She dashed to her vanity, grabbed her tweezers and a small jar of eye cream, placed the tick inside, and screwed the lid on tight.

Liz started to phone the detective but changed her mind. Spoke to her sister instead. Then Woo. Booked a flight to San Francisco the next morning. Woo could help her more than anyone at this point.

The next morning, Liz contacted her boss then stopped at a phone store on the way to the airport. She terminated her old phone number, got a new one. Later, she messaged the detective with her new phone number and told her she'd be away. Conover called her immediately. The FBI had found the entomologist in their database. "Many aliases and phony resumes. Moves around a lot. Arrested four times for stalking. Never jailed. Active in radical misogynist organizations."

"Is he my stalker?"

"Might be. We're looking at some other suspects, too."

"Is he still in this area?"

"We think he's in Phoenix."

"Is he stalking women all over the country?"

"Possibly."

Her skin prickled. He might have tried to kill her last night. She'd know soon enough. Had he poisoned other women? Maybe she should tell Conover what had happened.

"Has he ever harmed anyone?"

"Still too early in the investigation to know."

Too early? Your investigation is too friggin' slow, she thought. *I could be dead by the time you figure out who's after me and arrest him.*

—

Liz and Woo were on their way back from lunch when Liz mentioned she had captured her stalker's tick-bot and wanted to show it to him.

"You have it with you?"

"In an eye cream jar in my purse."

"You brought it across the country in your purse?"

She reached inside her handbag and held up the jar. "Can you take a look?"

He laughed and said, "Sure." When they got to the lab, he put it under the microscope.

"It's Russian. Has their signature injector and poison reservoir. The identification has been removed. Five or six years old."

"Is there poison in it?"

Woo increased the magnification. "Yep. Got to call the hazmat team." Liz's heart raced.

Minutes later, two people from hazmat were decontaminating everything in the lab, including her and Woo. They took the microscope, the tick, the eye cream jar, and Liz's purse for analysis and further decontamination. Said they'd call within an hour with the results.

Liz and Woo waited in his office, and she asked if she could see a bot's operating system again. She pulled her laptop from her tote, and soon, a spider-bot's system was up on Screen1. She switched control of the bot from Woo's phone number to hers, put the chip back into the spider, and drove it all over the lab. Her heart raced with excitement.

She asked where she could purchase the special flash drive, and Woo told her to keep the one in her laptop. Before she could thank him, his tile buzzed, and he excused himself to take the call. When he returned, he looked worried.

"It was Botox, Liz. A small but concentrated dose."

"Botox? Like the wrinkle treatment?"

"Yes. Botulinum toxin. The wrong dose can be lethal."

"Did the tick have enough to kill me?"

"Let's just say the Bug Stunner probably saved your life."

Liz swallowed hard, stared into space, processed confirmation of what she'd suspected. Woo asked if she wanted him to call her sister. Liz said no, she'd be fine. She didn't want to upset Sam.

"You're not going after this guy, are you?"

"No. But I may collect evidence."

"Be careful. He's obviously dangerous."

———

Two days later, Liz was at San Francisco International, waiting for a plane to Los Angeles. She had located the stalker in South Pasadena and booked three nights at the Beverly Hills Hilton. She'd fantasized over and over about giving her stalker a dose of his own medicine with his own tick-bot. But Liz knew committing murder would destroy her. Instead, her mission was to collect enough video evidence to put him in jail. Forever. She planned to send any evidence she gathered to the LAPD's anonymous tip line. Didn't want her name associated with any incriminating evidence against him. Feared other stalkers would target her.

She spent the next two days in her hotel room mastering the bot's capabilities on an untraceable, disposable smart-tile she purchased at the airport. Early her second evening in LA, she drove to South Pasadena. She wanted to verify that the entomologist was her stalker and figured dinnertime was the best time to snap a photo of him. Sure enough, the man who exited the door around seven was him. Same depraved eyes that had made her uncomfortable.

The next night was Liz's D-Day. She arrived early evening with the tick-bot in her purse and waited in the car until the stalker stepped out around six. He was nicely dressed, and she hoped he'd be out for a while. After he drove away, she steered the bot under his front door, parked it on a sofa leg just inside the entrance, then headed back to the hotel.

For the next two hours, her right leg jittered under her hotel room desk while she scouted the stalker's townhouse for evidence. What she saw filled her with rage and horror. One entire wall of his bedroom was devoted to photos of his victims, dozens of them. Most were taken in the victim's bathroom. Each one had a pink sticky note attached with the woman's name and address written with a black sharpie. She cringed when she saw a photo labeled *Liz*. It showed her stepping from the shower dripping wet, reaching for a towel.

As she panned the wall, she noticed something different about the photos in the middle. The women were all on the floor, in strange positions, as if they'd fallen out of bed. She zoomed in on the sticky notes in that section. Tears filled her eyes when she saw *R.I.P* written above each of their names. She wanted to throw up but forged ahead, filming every name and photo on the wall. Then she turned the bot's camera to the other bedroom walls. They were covered with ominous posters featuring brutal images of women. Each one screamed the name of an incendiary misogynist organization in large, bold letters.

Staving off waves of nausea, Liz moved the tick under the door to the second bedroom. It was obviously stalker central. Stacks of tiny boxes filled one bookcase with shelves labeled *houseflies, spiders, ticks, wasps, scorpions*. Dozens of disposable smart-tiles were piled neatly on another. Racks of bottles filled with liquids and powders hung over a small refrigerator with a large skull-and-bones decal on the door. A leather lounger sat in front of an oversized screen in the middle of the room. Two multi-screen laptops sat beside it.

It was after nine, and she needed to get the tick-bot out the door pronto. Her heart pounded as she drove the tick down the hall. She couldn't get the images of his victims out of her mind. Then, inches from the threshold, she heard the buzz of an electronic keypad. The serial killer was home. Her whole body trembled as she parked the tick on the sofa leg again. He burst through the door agitated, muttering under his breath, retrieved a photo from his bedroom, then stopped in the hall, shook his finger at it. "Tonight's your last night, bitch. You think you found me. But I found you first." He sniggered like a bully on a playground. Liz zoomed in on the photo. It was her. Dread twisted her gut. He stomped down the hall to stalker central and slammed the door.

Had he found her new phone number? Did he know where she was? What she was up to? Had she put herself in even more danger? Liz took a deep breath and steered the tick under the front door, down the outside walkway, to a trash bin next to the parking lot. From the top of the bin, she could see both the parking lot and the stalker's unit. Still trembling inside and out, she managed to compose her message to the LAPD anonymous tip hotline: "Urgent! Serial killer has murdered many women with poisonous insect bots (watch video). PLEASE go to (address). He's there."

Twenty long minutes later, Liz jumped when her tile dinged inside her purse on the bed. She opened the message, and her heart stopped as she read neon-green text. *Remember that chick in the shower in* Psycho? *You'll know what that feels like soon.* Shaking uncontrollably, she ran back to the desk, praying the cops were at his townhouse.

They weren't. Unable to suppress her nausea any longer, Liz grabbed both smart-tiles and dashed to the bathroom. She was washing her face when she heard the faint sound of sirens. She checked the disposable tile. Lights flashed in the distance, and the sirens grew louder. Soon lights flashed all over the parking lot, a SWAT team spilled from a van, and an FBI agent knocked on the door.

A pleasant warmth filled Liz's chest. She raised a hand to high-five herself in the mirror but stopped. A two-inch black wasp with red wings and a huge stinger crept along the top of the mirror. Then another buzzed her menacingly and landed on the countertop in front of her. She shrieked. Jumped back and fell over the vanity bench. As she scrambled to her feet, she heard buzzing above her and spied six more devil wasps on the bathroom ceiling and two more coming through an air vent. Running for the stunner wasn't an option. She pocketed both media tiles in her jeans, pulled all the towels from the racks, opened the glass shower door, and said, "maximum deluge." As warm water poured down on her, the buzzing intensified. A squadron of wasps descended on the glass walls surrounding her, crawled agitatedly on the outside, wiggling their stingers. She looked up and saw still more crawling from the air vent. Her heart felt like it might explode. She activated the hand shower with one hand, pulled her smart-tile from her pocket with the other, and dialed 911. Her breath caught repeatedly as she spoke to the dispatcher and hosed every wasp that crawled inside the shower. After she hung up, they kept coming. She tried to keep track of them as she hosed them down. Soon there were so many inside the shower she lost count.

HOpscOtch

Bernie Brown

Ginnie waited on her front steps for Elizabeth. As she studied the house where Marcie had lived, her stomach clenched in pain. Marcie used to play with them before she got sick and died. The girl had always insisted on having her own way. Their mothers made them include her. "Maybe she'll be nicer if you are nice to her." Their moms didn't know Marcie. Ginnie had heard her talk to her own parents. "Shut up, Mom," or "I'll eat in the car if I want to, Dad. What are you gonna do about it?"

Ginnie and Elizabeth included Marcie in hopscotch but not in sleepovers. Discussions about Marcie took place while they lounged on the bed eating popcorn. "She's a decent athlete but a terrible sport. She'd never make a team player."

"She isn't stupid, but she has a snotty attitude, even to the teachers."

"I feel sorry for her parents. They're so sweet and shy. Marcie was too much for them."

Ginnie and Elizabeth would stop talking about Marcie and polish each other's nails.

None of it really mattered now. She was dead.

———

"Hi! You ready to play?" Elizabeth stood in front of Ginnie, who looked up with a start.

"I was thinking about Marcie."

"I think about her, too." Elizabeth opened the box of chalk and drew the hopscotch squares in blue. Ginnie wrote in the numbers. "Remember how Marcie always wanted pink for the squares? She had pink everything."

"I guess it wouldn't hurt us to use pink once in a while," said Elizabeth.

"She'd probably come back from the dead and say something snotty like 'You're finally doing it right.'"

———

The squares were drawn, and the girls stood ready to play. "You go first," Ginnie said. Marcie had made them draw straws, and even then, she'd accuse them of cheating if she didn't draw the long one.

Last summer, the three girls had painted rocks to use as markers. Marcie's was pink, of course, with a flowery M that smudged together. It looked more like some strange animal's paw than an M. Ginnie painted a daisy, her favorite flower, and Elizabeth made a butterfly.

Elizabeth put her butterfly on square one, hopped over it, and made it safely to Home. On the return trip, she wobbled on square seven but then straightened, hopped, picked up her butterfly, and safely landed on Start.

"You were great catching yourself. I thought you were gonna put your foot down."

"I thought so, too. It was like somebody held me steady. So strange."

Ginnie shook her head. "Creepy." She tossed her daisy and got to Home and back with no trouble. "We're off to a good start."

When it was Ginnie's turn to throw on square four, her daisy landed on the line—something you lost your turn for—and then, it scooted back inside the square like somebody pushed it.

Elizabeth and Ginnie looked at each other, eyes wide. "I've never seen that happen before," said Elizabeth.

"Me, neither."

Elizabeth shook her head. "If Marcie had seen that, she would have said we cheated."

"If it happened on her turn, she wouldn't say a word."

"So true."

Thinking about what they had just seen made the girls pause.

At last, Ginnie shrugged and said, "I guess we keep on going."

They both made it to square ten without either having lost a turn.

"This is one weird game," said Elizabeth. "We've never had this kind of luck before. It's like somebody is helping us."

"It creeps me out. Let's finish as fast as we can and have some lemonade."

Elizabeth went smoothly from Start to Home, graceful as a dancer. When she stooped to pick up her butterfly, it was like taking a bow. She hopped back to Start. A perfect game.

Ginnie threw her daisy. It landed smack in the middle of the ten square. It didn't wiggle, bounce, or slide. Disbelief made her light-headed. She never made perfect throws.

She hopped directly to Home, jumping over ten. Once there, she took a deep breath. Would she get a perfect game, too?

She stooped to pick up her daisy and nicked it, so it slid away. She reached for it again, and it slid very near the line. When she reached again, she felt something hold her hand, place the daisy firmly inside, and close her fingers around it. Ginnie hadn't done it. Something or someone else had done it for her.

Ginnie hesitated before hopping back to Start, afraid she would break the spell if she made a mistake. As carefully as if she was hopping on hot coals, she made it, her daisy clutched tight in her hand.

Elizabeth waited for her, jumping up and down and applauding. "We've never done that before! Two perfect games. Like we're charmed."

Walking together back to the front steps, Ginnie asked, "I wonder what Marcie would have said. What if we had gotten three perfect games?"

"She would have said she won because she was first, or last, or in the middle. Whatever position was hers she would say was the winning position."

Elizabeth shrugged. "But she isn't here, and we are, and we did it together."

———

Ginnie's mom brought them big icy glasses of lemonade. As they sipped and giggled about their game, Ginnie stopped and asked, "Do you think Marcie ever regretted being so mean?"

Elizabeth didn't answer. As if hypnotized, she stared ahead at the lawn. She put down her glass and walked away a few slow, careful steps. Stooping, she picked up something hidden in the grass. She held out her find to Ginnie, whose mouth dropped open.

Elizabeth's hand held a dirty rock. Ginnie took it from her. She turned it over and over. Something pink lurked beneath the dirt, like a message.

Ginnie blew on the rock to rid it of dirt. The dirt remained. She rubbed it without success. She dipped her paper napkin in her lemonade and wiped the rock. The dirt vanished, and a splotchy pink M, like some strange animal's paw, shone clear and bright.

"Everyone has a monster inside." J.G. Faherty

The Halloween Hound

David Yurkovich

Every story has a beginning. Here's mine…

The western Maryland night air was cold and crisp as I readied my Schwinn, a three-speed Stingray model I'd gotten the year before for my tenth birthday, for the journey ahead. Halloween 1974 was going to be the night of the big haul. Massive haul. The haul-to-end-all-Halloween-hauls haul. No more walking through the neighborhood with my pals Mike and Brian, plodding along at pedestrian speed for three hours and returning home at the evening's end with bags barely one-third filled. No, this year, I had a plan.

It was simple math, something that my ten-year-old brain understood well enough. By bicycle, I could reach 72 more houses than I could on foot. Given the 1.4 ounce weight of a Hershey Bar, this meant an astonishing 6.3 additional pounds of candy, an astronomical feat for a boy of any age. I'd tried to convince my friends that this was the way to go, but both Mike and Brian scoffed at the idea. Tomorrow, they'd lament their decision.

The moonlight reflected the hands of my Timex: 6:30 p.m. Three hours would take me to 9:30, providing ample time to be home safe and sound before ten o'clock. It was a silly superstition, but everyone in town, young and old, believed in the legend of the Halloween Hound, a fierce beast alleged to roam the streets of Parksville after 10:00 p.m. each year on All Hallows' Eve in search of souls. Why especially Parksville? Your guess would be as good as mine. I've no doubt that most towns have their own mythologies, each invented, refined, and designed to elicit a particular response. Pure rubbish, though we, of course, all bought into it even if we said otherwise.

I climbed aboard my Schwinn, switched on the headlamp, positioned the dynamo against my front tire, and began pedaling. The headlamp began to glow, a narrow beacon slicing into the darkness. I was on my way.

In the ensuing hours, I raced up and down Parksville's narrow streets, passing by my foolish peers as they walked door to door, bags more than half empty. The plastic vampire teeth fit snugly in my mouth, and my cape floated in the air behind me like a thing alive. The plastic bag, an orange and black necessity purchased earlier in the month from the Hatsbridge Five and Dime, grew heavier each minute. It hung from the right handlebar of my three-speed, and I held it firmly for extra protection, but balancing the Schwinn against this added weight was challenging. The bike consistently pulled right, though I soon adjusted and was able to maintain a decent speed.

The Timex read 8:45. So much time remaining. I pedaled away from the main drag and over toward the rowhomes that, before Parksville's coal supply ran out, had been occupied by the mine workers. I didn't know the area well, but candy was a sweet siren not to be ignored.

Eleven blocks later, I arrived at Hyde Street, adjusted my cape, and approached the first house on the block. The face that greeted me was as sour as a December Granny Smith apple.

"Trick or Treat!" I exclaimed, with more than a bit of trepidation.

"Go home, kid. Halloween's over," the grayish man replied through the screen door.

"It's not even," I blurted.

From within the stranger's house, a grandfather clock began to chime. I counted the tolls of the clock—all ten of them—and then glanced at my Timex: 8:45. Only then did I notice that the sweep hand was not advancing.

"Get on home; it's late. Be careful now." He closed the door and switched off the porch light.

Glancing left to right, I became keenly aware of the darkness of the street and the accompanying silence. Ten o'clock! Go! Go now! I dashed toward the Schwinn and leaped aboard the banana seat, slammed my right foot against the kickstand, and dropped both feet onto the pedals. By all estimates, I was 15 minutes from home. I hooked my bag, which was filled to near bursting, over the right handlebar. But any feelings of pride at this amazing Halloween haul were suppressed by my increasing panic. *It's only a stupid legend; it's not real,* I reminded myself.

After what felt like an eternity, legs pumping to exhaustion and a waterfall of perspiration cascading down the nape of my neck, I reached my familiar neighborhood streets. Four blocks 'til home. I hung a left onto Beaker Street, still moving at a good clip.

The dog appeared out of nowhere, resting low to the ground beneath a distant streetlight. I knew all the animals in the neighborhood, but this was one I'd never seen before. It wasn't massive but was mid-sized at best. It was a stray. Nothing to worry about. One fact was immediately apparent: the creature did not like me. As I sped along Walnut Street, it rose from the cold ground and seemed to double in size. White smoke trailed from its nostrils as its eyes, ghastly crimson orbs, met mine. What little strength remained in my legs seemed to evaporate, and my bike slowed as I rolled ever closer toward what was certainly the Halloween Hound.

The cur snarled incessantly, sound reverberating up and down an otherwise silent street, and it charged toward me. Panicked, I found sudden resolve and began to pedal with renewed vigor. The Schwinn teetered side to side, still unbalanced by the weight of my night's work. The bike's headlamp radiated brighter as my speed increased. But the mongrel, legs effortlessly bounding atop the pavement, proved more than my equal. The beast was soon by my side. I turned onto Cherry Street. Glancing down, I gasped at the exposed silver fangs within arm's reach. Suddenly it leaped into the air.

It scarcely missed my right leg, finding instead the trick-or-treat bag housing my precious cargo. The plastic was ripped open in seconds, a large gash that resulted in half of my boon falling immediately onto the street. It struck a second time, again tearing at the candy bag. The Schwinn straightened, free of the weight that had previously unbalanced it. My speed escalated, and the indignant canine, for reasons I will likely never know, suddenly abandoned its pursuit. Moments later, I reached my home and jumped from the Schwinn. As the bike skidded to the ground, I hurried inside, clutching a largely empty bag, and deadbolted the door.

I peeked out the window several times, seeing only the distant glow of Jack-o-lanterns. I soon reasoned that in all likelihood, the animal that had given chase was merely a stray, and the rest had been the product of my imagination. Still, stray or not, it had been a costly encounter. I spat plastic fangs into the trash and poured what remained of my haul onto the kitchen table. The entire lot consisted of a few Hershey Bars and a Kit-Kat. Pathetic.

"You're home late," Mom said, as she stepped into the kitchen. "How'd it go?"

"Don't sneak up like that!" I said, startled. "Anyway, can't say that it went well at all."

"I'm sorry, sweetie. If it's any consolation, there's plenty of leftover candy in the jar. We always buy too much. Lights out in fifteen, okay?"

"Okay, Mom."

Alone again, I held my trick-or-treat bag and examined the two holes through which the bulk of my bounty had vanished. The hound's fangs had clearly caused the damage, but the bag itself appeared to have been partially melted. I ran a finger along the outline of one of the gashes and quickly pulled my hand away from what I can only describe as a blistering frigidity. Within seconds the empty plastic sack felt heavy in my hands. I dropped the bag, and it shattered into several dozen pieces on the kitchen floor.

I wanted to run but instead retrieved a broom and dustpan to collect the mess. It decomposed before my eyes, and within moments, all that remained was dust, which I quickly swept up. Once done, I removed the candy bars from the kitchen table and tossed them in the trash.

I passed by the candy jar in the living room and removed a few of my favorites—3 Musketeers, Mounds, Reese's Peanut Butter Cups—devouring them in my room as I changed into pajamas. It all tasted bitter, and I'd had enough of this night. Minutes later, I brushed my teeth before falling asleep reading the adventures of Captain America.

Early the next morning, I returned to the scene of the attack, determined to find evidence that would validate the terror I'd experienced. All that remained were scattered ashes of candy bar wrappers which, although curious, proved nothing.

I shared the tale later that day with Mike and Brian, describing in full detail the physical and supernatural characteristics of the Halloween Hound. My friends issued a look of sarcasm.

"What did ya expect?" Mike said, shaking his head.

"Yeah, stupid," Brian added. "You break the rules, you pay a price."

The following Halloween, we walked together, a trio of eleven-year-old ghosts navigating our neighborhood streets on an unusually mild October night. Mike, Brian, and I parted ways at 9:15, a bit earlier than usual, but that was okay. Following the brief walk home, I dove headlong into a sugar rush produced by a partially full bag of treats. Snuggled in my bed, I heard a distant, unearthly howl. The Timex read ten o'clock.

"Not this year," I said, pulling my bag of candy to my chest and embracing the joys and terrors of the witching season.

UNwell

Faye Perozich

She didn't know if she could do it.

It wasn't that she'd had a change of heart; ever since the accident that had claimed the life of her fiancé, she had wanted to commit suicide. It was *all* she wanted. When she woke each morning, it was her first thought of the day; when she went to bed each night, she quietly prayed for a mid-sleep aneurysm that would take the decision out of her hands. Just six months earlier, she'd been planning a whole new life—a happy life, a life that felt full of love and promise. And suddenly, her plans were gone, Scott was gone, and the promise of that happy life was shattered.

Yes, she wanted to die. And now she finally knew how she wanted to do it. Yet, she still didn't know if she could really go through with it.

Because it would kill her father.

"Jessie? You with me?"

"Yeah, Dad."

She didn't look up at him. Side by side, they were crossing the expanse of yard behind their house, heading for the old well. It was already within sight, a ramshackle blemish amid the line of poplars that marked the northern edge of the property.

"Seems like you're someplace else."

"Just thinking," Jessie sighed. It wasn't a lie. "Why'd you want to take the cover off that thing today, anyway?"

"I told you," Christopher Whitt replied. "I've got to get it filled in, as it should be. It's too dangerous to just leave as it is. The top is crumbling, and the damn thing's so deep—"

"Yeah, I know all that," Jessie interrupted. "But why do you want to do it *now?* That well hasn't seen water in twenty years, so what's the rush?"

Not that she was sorry he'd decided to do it. She'd been wanting to kill herself for almost six months, but she didn't know how to do it in a way that would guarantee she'd wind up in the morgue instead of waking up in a hospital on a psychiatric hold. It was only when her father had mentioned uncovering and filling in the old well that she'd finally decided on a plan.

"Needs to be done," Christopher said, shrugging. "Now, a year from now … I just figured I'd get it done while I still can. The old ticker might not be up to it next year."

She finally looked up at him. She loved him; she truly *did* still love him, despite everything that had happened. True, she blamed him, but reproach didn't negate love.

"Don't say that, Dad."

"Don't worry," he replied, smiling. "Everything is as it should be."

"Is your heart giving you trouble again?"

"No more than usual, hon," he said, shrugging his shoulders again. "Gets a little cranky when I exert myself, but that's what I've got the pills for."

"So here you go, exerting yourself," Jessie said, shaking her head. "Real smart."

Christopher let out a little laugh and patted the front pocket of his old jeans, the ratty ones he always wore when he worked in the yard.

"Got my nitro right here," he said, giving her a playful nudge with his elbow. "Got *you* here, too."

"Nitroglycerin might not save you one of these days," she said, looking back down at her feet. "And I don't know how much help I'll be, either. You yourself always say that I'm as light as a feather."

"I just need a little extra force," he said. "Even the force of a feather should work! You can do it, hon."

Now it was Jessie who shrugged. She'd never been a strong person, physically or emotionally, and they both knew it. But she thought that, maybe, she really *could* help this time.

She was certainly determined to give it her all.

The grass had grown high around the well, mixing with the weeds to create an unsightly border around the circle of old stone. The conical roof was still held in place by two sturdy beams, but some of the boards from the roof had fallen away over the years, giving it the appearance of a gap-toothed grin. To Jessie, it seemed a truly eerie smile, yet somehow inviting.

A pulley still hung from another sturdy beam beneath the roof, supporting a length of rope; one end of the rope was coiled on top of the well's cover, while the other end snaked over the side of the well and disappeared into the weeds below.

Christopher Whitt barely took notice of the rope as he studied the heavy wooden cover; he simply pushed the coiled end off to the side as he attempted to mentally calculate the weight of the lid.

"Shouldn't be too tough," he said, although he sounded very unsure. "But this is the first time I wish I'd had a son!"

Jessie bristled immediately. Her mind was suddenly filled with every instance in which her father had called Scott "son" during their all-too-brief engagement.

"You could have *had* a son," she said. Her teeth clenched as she spoke, as did her fists.

She knew it had been a joke. She knew he didn't mean anything by it. She knew he already regretted saying it. But she didn't care. She was hurt, she was angry, and she was blaming him all over again. It was his own fault that he didn't have a "son" to help him right now. It was his fault that Scott was dead.

And for a split second—although it felt much, much longer than that to Jessie—it was perfectly all right with her that what she had planned would kill him.

"Oh, Jessie, honey, I didn't—"

"Forget it." Cold, abrupt. "Let's just get this done."

"Are you okay?"

"Fine."

They both knew it was a lie.

Jessie stared at the well cover. She could feel her father's eyes on her, and she couldn't bear to meet them. When she saw him take a step toward her, she moved quickly out of reach; she could bear his touch even less than his gaze. Instead, she stepped up to the well and began to push on the cover by herself. It wouldn't budge, but that didn't keep her from throwing all of her might into it.

Wrestling against all of the things he wanted to say, Christopher stepped up next to his daughter in silence. He placed his hands next to hers on the wooden cover and started to push. He'd thought of the chore as something they could do together, father and daughter, but now it felt like they were two complete strangers who just happened to be in the same place, each doing the same thing by sheer coincidence, an entire world of loneliness, guilt, and grief separating them.

Lost in thought, Jessie barely noticed her father's presence beside her, scarcely felt it when the cover began to move.

A cougar is what she thought, as she had thought every day for the past six months.

A fucking cougar, of all things.

The camping trip had been her father's idea, and perhaps that was reason enough for Jessie to blame him.

It was a bonding thing; Christopher Whitt had said that if his daughter was going to spend the rest of her life with this guy, then they should get to know each other better. He'd said that was as it should be. And to Christopher, who had always loved the outdoors, that meant one thing: camping. Jessie had wanted to go along—she'd gone camping in the hills with her father many times before—but her father had refused, saying that her presence would defeat the whole purpose of the trip. That had been strike two against her father; Jessie would spend the next six months tortured by the thought that things might have turned out differently, somehow, if only she'd gone with them.

It had happened on the very first night. Scott must have needed to urinate sometime in the middle of the night. He hadn't gone far; the rangers had found the first signs of a struggle—not to mention a pool of coagulated blood— just ten feet from the tent.

Christopher, who'd been sleeping soundly in the tent, had heard nothing. Strike three.

Her father had called the rangers as soon as he woke and realized that Scott was gone; the rangers had called in a rescue team to search the hills after they discovered the blood and cougar tracks behind the tent. They'd found seven pieces of Scott in all, making up less than a quarter of his body. His head had been found over a mile away from the campsite.

And though she never saw those pieces of Scott's body, Jessie had always imagined that Scott's eyes were open and staring, his mouth twisted in a tormented scream.

Had he screamed? Jessie couldn't believe that her father didn't hear such a brutal attack. The rangers had explained to her, delicately, that Scott had probably been taken by surprise and perhaps had never had the chance to scream. Or perhaps the cougar had gone for his throat in that very first lunge, making it impossible for Scott to cry out.

Jessie had nodded her understanding to the rangers, but she really didn't understand, *couldn't* understand. Her father had been sleeping in the same tent, yet he hadn't heard Scott stir, hadn't heard him leave, hadn't heard him being viciously attacked just ten feet away. It simply didn't make sense to her, then or now.

And so, yes, she blamed her father for Scott's death. Christopher Whitt hadn't planned the attack; he didn't even know there were cougars in those hills. He had wished Scott no harm, and simply sleeping made him guilty of nothing. All of that was true. Yet, to Jessie, he was completely responsible. And though she sincerely loved her father, the feeling that he was to blame for everything that had gone wrong in her life never went away.

—

By the time they pushed the cover all the way off the well, they were both huffing for air. Jessie bent over, placing her hands on her knees, trying to catch her breath. She saw her father out of the corner of her eye; he seemed to be truly struggling to breathe.

"You okay, Dad?"

Christopher nodded but didn't reply. He reflexively placed one hand on his chest, over his heart; Jessie could almost hear it pounding beneath his sweat-soaked tee.

"Better take a pill."

He nodded again, reaching into the pocket of his old jeans. He pulled out a small silver tube, a birthday gift from his daughter the year before. He had always complained that the prescription bottle his pills came in was too big for his pocket, so Jessie had gotten him the silver tube; it was less than two inches long and only the width of a pinky finger—plenty small enough to fit in his pocket, but large enough to hold more than a dozen of his tiny nitroglycerin pills.

Christopher shook one of the pills out of the tube and placed it under his tongue, and they both waited in silence for the medicine to work its magic.

When Jessie finally regained her breath, and Christopher's heart stopped hammering in his chest, they stepped up to the well again and peered in. They could only see down a dozen feet or so; beyond that, sunlight could not penetrate.

"I think we're going to need a flashlight," Christopher mused, "though I don't think I've got one bright enough to reach all the way to the bottom."

"How deep is it?" Jessie asked. She hoped that her voice wouldn't betray her eagerness; as she stared down into the well, straining to see as much as she could, the black void below her seemed to be beckoning.

"No idea. Pretty sure it's at least fifty feet, though it could be twice that."

"Wow! Are you sure there's no water?"

"Why?" Christopher said, giving a little chuckle. "You thirsty?"

"Actually, yeah," she replied, and now she laughed, too. "But I was thinking lemonade, not well water."

"That's as it should be!" he said, clapping the dirt from his hands. "Lemonade sounds good to me—let's go get some." He paused. "And Jessie?"

She finally stopped staring into the inky pit and looked up at him, and another wave of misgiving washed over her. God help her—she *did* still love him.

"Yes?"

"Thanks for the help," he said. "The concrete to fill it in will be here tomorrow, and I don't think I would have gotten the damn cover off without you."

"I was happy to help," Jessie replied, and it was true.

—

Later that night, Jessie returned to the well. But she stopped at her father's bedroom first.

Christopher Whitt was sleeping, and he didn't hear her open the door. She watched him from the doorway for a few long moments, battling with her doubts again; how could she even *think* of hurting him this way, when he'd done nothing that was really wrong? She supposed that what she was planning could be murder, in a sense, but she couldn't bear to think of it that way. Each time she thought of it as murder, her mind shut down; something in her brain stopped, backed up, and rewound to a point where it wasn't murder, it was suicide, only suicide, and isn't that what she'd longed for all this time? Her life had become a haunted thing, and she didn't want to live it anymore.

And there was nothing wrong with that, was there?

She saw his old jeans draped over a chair beside his bed, and she stepped into the room. She was sure that he would stir, but he slept on. He didn't hear her leave his room, didn't hear her close the back door, didn't hear her make her way through the yard to the well.

Part of her still hoped that she wouldn't need the last piece of her plan. Certainly, the fall alone would be enough to kill her, and nothing more would be necessary; in her dark tomb, it wouldn't matter if he found her right away or if he didn't figure it out until the well was filled in. It certainly wouldn't matter to *her*.

But the part of her that had become angry and bitter after Scott's death— the part of her that still blamed Christopher Whitt for everything that had gone wrong in her life—was morbidly pleased that her father hadn't noticed that the rope had been brand new.

That part of her hoped that she would need to use it.

—

Christopher Whitt was having the same dream he always had these days, where someone was screaming in agony, and he was frozen in fear. But something was off; the scream was different this time.

Dad!

Jessie was suddenly there in the dream, somewhere, calling out to him, but she couldn't be there. Something wasn't right. He'd told her not to come; why was she there?

"Dad!"

He rose slowly through his dream, trying to make sense of what was happening, but the threads of the dream were already beginning to break. He was left stranded for a moment, stuck in that peculiar state that was no longer a dream but not yet full consciousness. He heard her call out again.

"Dad!"

It was definitely his daughter's voice, but it seemed to be coming from the other side of the world. Was he still dreaming?

"Dad! Help me!"

He was awake in an instant then, the dream gone, the remnants of it already forgotten. Reality was suddenly clear; he was in his bed, dawn was slipping through the part in the curtains, and his daughter needed help.

"Jessie?"

There was no reply. He got out of bed, trying to figure out where her voice was coming from. The odd sound of it frightened him. He grabbed the clothes he'd worn the previous day and wriggled into them as he made his way to the bedroom door.

"Jessie?" he called, a little louder this time. "Where are you?"

"Dad!"

She was still calling out, but she hadn't heard him. She wasn't in the house; he could tell that much. He went to the front door and threw it open, but then he heard her voice again, and he realized that it was coming from somewhere in the backyard. He ran around the side of the house, calling to her again, louder still.

"Jessie! Where are you?"

"The well!"

He froze.

Oh my God, he thought, his heart leaping in his chest. *Not that. Not the well.*

He paused only a second, then ran to the well as fast as he could. He looked down into it, but there was only darkness, and he chastised himself for not grabbing a flashlight.

"Dad!" Jessie called up, her voice loud in the echo chamber of rock. "You heard me!"

"Oh God, Jessie! What the hell happened?"

She was crying now, softly, but he could hear each hitch of her chest clearly.

"I'm sorry, Dad," she said. "I lost my engagement ring, and I thought I must have dropped it when we took the cover off the well. I came out here … it was dark … Oh, Dad, I'm so sorry!"

"Are you hurt?"

"My legs," she replied, "they're broken pretty badly. Oh, Dad, get me out of here!"

"I'll go call 911!" he shouted down. "You just wait—"

"No!" she screamed. Her voice was filled with panic, and it tore at his heart.

"No, please don't leave me, Dad! *Please!*"

"It's okay, honey," he said, trying to make his voice sound calm and soothing, straining to keep his own panic veiled. "It's okay. I'm right here! But I have to go and get help!"

"No!" she screamed again, sobbing harder. "No, please! I've been alone down here all night. I can't stand it anymore! Just throw down the rope—you can pull me up!"

Christopher looked at the rope, still coiled on the rim of the well, and wondered if such a thing were possible.

"I don't think …"

"Come on, Dad! You can do it! You always say I'm light as a feather! You can help me. You can get me out of here!"

He placed one hand on the rope, wrestling with his thoughts. The rope looked strong enough; in fact, it looked brand new. But was *he* strong enough?

"Come on, Dad! Don't let me down!"

And with that, the decision was made. He *could* do it. He could pull her out. She was his daughter, and she needed his help, and hadn't he already let her down enough?

Resolute, Christopher grabbed the rope. He could see the other end lying in the tall grass that circled the well; he put his foot on it, anchoring that end, and readied the coiled end over the well.

"Jessie?" he called. "I'm going to throw the rope down now. Get ready!"

"I'm ready, Dad," she replied, the panic gone from her voice now. Christopher mistook it as relief.

"Here it comes!"

He dropped the rope into the well and watched it disappear into the blackness. He fought against his doubts, hoping that the rope was long enough to reach her, not knowing what he would do if it wasn't. Angry at himself for not picking up his cell phone before he left the house. It seemed to take forever for the rope to reach her. He waited impatiently, his thoughts feeding on his fears.

She finally called out: "Got it!"

"Okay, honey. Now, tie it around your waist and hold on to the rope. Make sure it's a strong knot! Then I'll pull you up!"

Doubt, again. He didn't know if he could do it. True, his daughter weighed next to nothing, and apart from the occasional flutter of his heart, he was in good shape. He certainly *felt* strong enough. Still …

"Okay, it's tied!" Jessie called. "Pull me up!"

His doubts were trying to stop him, but he couldn't allow that to happen. He couldn't let his fear take control, not again, not now. His daughter needed him. He *had* to save her.

Yes, he would save her, and then he would fix things; he would fix all of the things that had gone wrong between them. He would make things better for Jessie and for himself; he would make things *right* again. And then, perhaps, she wouldn't be so sad anymore, and he would never feel the crushing weight of guilt again.

All he had to do was pull her out of the well. Then everything would be all right. Everything would be as it should be.

"Dad?"

"Yes, I'm here!"

"I love you."

He started to cry. He didn't know why; he hadn't shed tears for a very long time. He decided that he was simply overwhelmed.

"I love you, too, Jessie," he said, and he started to pull.

It took him almost twenty minutes to hoist her to the top of the well. He had to pause several times to catch his breath, but he never lost his determination. He remained hopeful about the future right up until he pulled her all the way to the top, but when he finally saw her, he understood immediately that he would never be able to fix all of the things that had gone wrong between them. Nothing would ever make things better; nothing would ever make things right.

She'd tied the rope around her neck.

Christopher stood and stared at her, his heart shattered.

Jessie's eyes were open. She seemed to be staring at him, but he couldn't tell if she was seeing him or not. Tears still stained her cheeks; her mouth was open, as if she were just about to speak. Her hands were balled into two tight fists, and her legs dangled below her body at crazy angles. They were both fractured in so many places that she looked like a broken marionette, frozen in the midst of some elaborate dance.

He'd killed her. He'd hung his own daughter.

"Oh, Jessie …"

He couldn't bear to let go of the rope. She would drop back down, into the well, and he couldn't stand the idea of his precious daughter being in that dark pit, not for another second. So he held on to the rope, not really sure of what to do next, not even wanting to think that far ahead.

"Jessie …"

Once again, Christopher reflexively placed a hand on his chest; his heart was thumping wildly. And suddenly, the pain was increasing, growing unbearable far too quickly. He realized that this was more than angina; he'd had one heart attack already, and he knew the feeling. The pain in his chest … his back … his arm … his jaw. He reached into the pocket of his ratty old jeans, but the pills weren't there. He must have lost the little silver tube Jessie had given him. He looked around him in the grass but gave up the search quickly; he realized that he could have lost it anywhere. It might have slipped out of the pocket when he'd thrown his jeans on the chair the night before. Searching would be useless.

Oh well, he thought. *That's all right.*

Christopher dropped to his knees. He was still holding the rope tightly in one hand, and when he fell to the ground, Jessie's body jerked, her legs flailing for a few seconds in a macabre ballet. He clutched the rope with both hands now, holding it to his chest, feeling his heart pound against his breastbone. The pain was getting worse, doubling impossibly with each passing moment, becoming agony. And though he knew it was just past dawn, the sun seemed to be going down already. And that was as it should be, he thought, because he was getting very, very tired.

He laid down on his side, and the grass felt cool on his cheek; it was a pleasant sensation, and he felt grateful for it. He could still see Jessie, his beautiful Jessie; as he watched her, he saw that her muscles were relaxing, and he knew that they were dying, both dying, right this minute, father and daughter, dying together. He watched as the lines in her face went slack; he watched as, one after the other, her fists slowly opened and her fingers went limp. He watched as the little silver tube glittered for a second in the morning sun, then rolled out of her hand and fell down into the well.

Christopher Whitt sighed and closed his eyes. He knew that his Jessie was no longer sad, and he knew that he would never have to feel the crushing weight of guilt again.

And that was as it should be.

"stare at the dark too long and you will eventually see what isn't there."

cameron jace

Into the Fire

David W. Dutton

The sudden knocking startled Carol Maitland. She jumped and turned from the sink to face the French doors that led from her kitchen to the side porch. Her neighbor, Anne Guthrie, smiled and waved at her. Carol returned the smile and motioned for Anne to enter.

Carol and her husband, Brad, had recently purchased the rambling Victorian farmhouse from Anne and her husband, Frank. The big, old house had become too much for the Guthries once their children had grown and moved on with their lives. They opted to build a smaller, more convenient dwelling on an adjoining property. The Guthries were old friends of Carol's parents, so they negotiated the sale of the house directly with Carol and Brad rather than through a realtor.

Anne closed the door behind her. "Sorry to startle you. Is this a bad time?"

Carol laughed. "Of course not. I just brewed a new pot. Want a cup?"

"Certainly."

"It's hazelnut. I hope that's all right." Carol motioned to the row of stools that flanked the far side of the big island. "Sit."

Anne did as directed. "Hazelnut is fine."

As Carol busied herself with the coffee, Anne looked around the big country kitchen. "I can't believe you thought to paint the cabinets. The blue is so much softer than the dark walnut. Wish I had thought of that."

"I'm glad you approve." Carol set a mug in front of her neighbor, followed by cream and sugar.

Anne raised a hand. "I'm fine, thanks. I like it just the way it is." She sipped the strong brew.

Carol leaned against the side of the island and cradled her mug in her hands. "So, what's up with your day?"

Anne laughed. "Not much. Frank's off in pursuit of the little white ball, so I've got the day to myself. You?"

"Trying to convince myself to finally finish unpacking the last five boxes. I'm tired of seeing them stacked in the foyer."

Anne nodded. "You've done a lot in two months. It's hard to believe you've gotten so much accomplished in so little time."

"Seems to me it's taken forever."

"I'm sure it does. Moving a family of four is no small feat." Carol smiled and nodded.

"The children seem to have settled in well."

"Oh, yes. They love the house … love their new rooms."

The Maitland siblings numbered two. Fourteen-year-old Renee was the elder; her brother, Clark, was twelve. Because her parents had opted for the original second-floor master suite, Renee had claimed the first-floor master that the Guthries had added to the house years earlier. Clark chose the big bedroom at the end of the rear wing, a good distance from his parents.

A sudden tortured screeching of wood on metal startled Carol and Anne. They stared at the bank of three windows above the sink as the center unit slid quickly upward.

"Damn!" Carol crossed to the sink, pulled down the sash, and locked it. "That's been happening a lot lately. I've asked Brad to look at it, but he hasn't had time." She turned back to face Anne. "Was that a problem when you lived here?"

Anne sighed and nodded. "Yes, I'm afraid so."

Carol laughed. "Scares the bejesus out of me every time."

Anne took a deep breath. "Well … that's part of the reason I stopped by this morning."

"To discuss my kitchen window?"

"That, and a couple of other things." Anne patted the stool next to her. "Come sit by me. This may take a while."

Uncertainty gripped the young mother as she rounded the island and slid onto the stool next to her neighbor. Anne's tone was troubling. Carol wasn't sure she wanted to hear what Anne had to say.

"So? What is this about my window?" Carol asked, feigning a carefree laugh.

Anne stared at Carol over her coffee mug. "I'm afraid I … we …. haven't been completely honest with you."

"In what way?"

"We should have told you before we ever entered into negotiations. Now, I'm feeling guilty that we didn't."

"I don't understand. We love the house. It's exactly what we were looking for. I can't imagine anything that would have kept us from buying it."

Anne set her mug on the island with a sharp thud. "It's haunted."

Carol stifled a laugh. "It's what?"

"Haunted. It has ghosts. Three of them."

Carol found the pronouncement somewhat amusing, but she also felt a tendril of dread begin to insinuate itself. She didn't consider herself a skeptic. She had read and heard of too many accounts to dismiss supernatural claims as pure imagination. Deep inside, she knew Anne was telling the truth.

"Three of them," Carol said.

Anne nodded. "A family … husband, wife, and daughter."

An audible gasp escaped Carol. "Really?"

"Yes. They built the house and lived here until, well, the end."

"The end?"

Anne reached out and laid her hand on Carol's. "Forgive me. I'm being too dramatic." She sighed. "It's a sad story."

Carol remained silent. She already knew more than she wanted, but she also knew that her neighbor was not going to stop until she had totally unburdened herself.

"Apparently, everything was fine until the pandemic of 1918. Their daughter, who was ten, died of influenza. The parents were understandably devastated. The mother never recovered. She died one year later of what was described as a broken heart. The husband continued to live here but became a raging alcoholic. One day, after an especially long bout of drinking, he staggered down the road and drowned himself in Paynter's Pond."

"That's horrible!" Carol looked at Anne in shock. "Are you sure?"

Anne nodded solemnly. "That's the accepted story that's been passed along all these years."

"My God. Wait until Brad hears about this."

90

"I'm so sorry. We should have told you, but Frank has never been fully convinced that there's any truth to the story or the haunting."

"But you are?"

Anne nodded again. "Yes. I've seen and experienced too much. They're here. Of that, I'm certain."

"The window?"

"Yes, but more than that." Anne inhaled deeply before continuing. "The smell of lavender is frequently present. I assume it was the mother's perfume. There are cold spots from time to time, especially in the hallway of the rear wing. I've heard rustlings in the attic that were only audible from the second floor." Anne paused to chuckle. "I think our cats became aware of their presence first."

"How so?"

"I noticed it soon after we finished remodeling. The house had been quiet up until then, or, at least, if there was any activity, it wasn't immediately noticeable. After we relocated the stairs to allow for the master suite addition, the cats seemed to develop a fascination with the stairway." Anne motioned to the open steps that separated the country kitchen from the more formal rooms at the front of the house. "They would laze about, as cats do, and then suddenly stare up at the top of the stairs. I watched their eyes follow something … or someone … as they'd descended the stairwell."

"That's … bizarre, even by cat standards."

"It worked in reverse as well. Up or down, the cats always seemed attuned to what was happening."

A chill passed down Carol's spine. She took a deep breath. "I've watched Maggie act the same way. I never thought I'd be creeped out by our pooch, but it was creepy."

"Animals are very sensitive," Anne said. "A lot more so than us."

Carol nodded thoughtfully. "I suppose." She paused before continuing. "Have you ever actually seen them? The ghosts, I mean."

Anne paused. "I saw the husband and wife once. There was no sign of their little girl. Usually, the disturbances consisted of random sounds or a feeling that indicated their presence."

"How do you know the daughter is here if you've never seen her?"

"The legend, of course, and a couple of … occurrences … involving our children."

"Really?"

"Both our boys claimed to hear the voice of a little girl from time to time. This was right after the remodel and the increase in strange activity. Usually occurred at night, after they'd gone to bed. They shared the big bedroom at the end of the hall. Anyway, at first, I dismissed it."

"What changed your mind?"

Anne laughed lightly. "Well, she wouldn't stop. At first, it was once or twice a month. Then it escalated to weekly. Frank and I grew weary of the boys waking us up, so we finally moved them into the second-floor master bedroom. After that, I guess the poor thing didn't know where they had gone."

Carol shivered. "That goes right through me. Sorry. But when did you see the parents?"

"I was working here in the kitchen when I heard a noise from the foyer. I walked over to the doorway and looked to the cause. They were both seated on my French Provincial love seat."

"The red one? Yes, I remember it."

"They were dressed as you might expect. They held hands, stared straight ahead, never moving. I stared at them for several seconds before they simply disappeared."

Carol clasped her right hand to her chest. "My God! That would have scared me to death."

Anne laughed. "Actually, I was quite calm. I returned to the kitchen and finished emptying the dishwasher."

"And you never saw them again?"

"No, but I'm certain they continued to sit on the love seat from time to time. I'd often notice that the feather cushions had been flattened down. It became a habit for me to continually re-fluff them."

"That's wild."

"As I said, I'm sorry to burden you with this. We should have told you much sooner." Carol picked up her coffee mug.

"No. That's okay. I mean, it's not like they're evil or anything." She stared at her neighbor askance. "I'm right, aren't I?"

Anne smiled. "They've always appeared perfectly harmless ... sad more than anything."

"It's a sad tale."

"Right before you moved in, I went up to the attic where I've often felt their presence. I told them we were leaving but that a nice new family would soon be living with them."

Carol laughed. "That was kind of you. What did they say about that?"

Anne joined in the laughter. "I'll let you discover the answer to that question."

—

"That's quite a tale." Brad Maitland speared half a meatball with his fork and popped it into his mouth.

Fourteen-year-old Renee stared at her father. "I think it's scary."

"That's because you read Stephen King," her twelve-year-old brother, Clark, said, his tone revealing skepticism as he toyed with his pasta.

Carol laughed. "Enough, you two. I'm only repeating what Mrs. Guthrie told me."

Clark snorted. "She's an old woman. Probably just her imagination."

"Clark! That's not nice." Renee glared at her brother across the table. "Mrs. Guthrie has always been kind to us."

"Even so, she could have an overactive imagination."

Brad laid aside his fork. "Enough, Clark. It's a story ... a legend. We've no way to know if it's true or not."

Renee looked to her mother for support. "You talked to her, Mom. Did it sound like it was her imagination?"

Carol sighed. "No, dear. She seemed very definite about what she was saying and believed they were real."

"We haven't experienced anything unusual." Clark looked from his sister to his parents. "Have we?"

Carol smiled. "There's the window."

"It's a window, Mom," Clark said. "Windows open and close."

Renee glared at her brother. "By themselves?"

Brad swallowed a sip of wine. "They're spring-loaded, so it's possible."

"Have you seen or heard anything?" Clark pushed aside his empty plate.

Brad's silence blanketed the table. "The other night, I was working late in my office ..." He paused.

Carol glanced at her husband in surprise. "And?"

"I became suddenly aware of a scent. It was ... powerful. Potent."

"A scent?" Carol asked. "What sort of scent?"

"Lavender."

—

The rest of the week unfolded without fanfare. Clark remained skeptical, and Renee continued to feel apprehensive. Carol and Brad's lives were status quo.

Everything changed the following week.

The sudden opening of their bedroom door awakened Carol. She sat up in bed, confused but aware that something wasn't right. She stared at the form outlined by the hallway light.

"Mom?" Clark called out, voice muffled and filled with uncertainty. "Mom? You awake?"

Carol threw back the covers and swung her feet off the side of the bed. "What is it, honey?"

Clark entered the darkened bedroom. "I'm scared."

Carol reached toward the nightstand and switched on the lamp. A soft glow filled the corner of the chamber.

As Clark ran across the room, Brad roused from his slumber. He squinted at the sudden light. "What's wrong?"

Carol's son jumped onto the bed and wrapped both arms around his mother.

"I'm not sure." Clark's face was buried against his mom.

Carol glanced over Clark's shoulder at her husband and restated her question. "What's the matter, honey?"

The boy simply shook his head.

"Hey, Sport." Brad gently caressed Clark's shoulder. "What's happened?"

"Someone's in my room."

"Are you sure?"

Clark nodded forcefully.

"I'll go take a look." Brad, now fully awake, rose from the bed and walked quickly from the room and down the long hallway of the rear wing.

He returned minutes later. "There's no one there. I searched under the bed and in the closet. The windows are locked tight. I also searched the rest of the house. No sign of anyone. Even Maggie's fast asleep on the sofa, and she'd definitely have barked if someone unknown was here." Brad sat on the bed beside his wife and son. "You had a bad dream. That's all."

There was a moment of silence before Clark responded. "It wasn't a dream. I heard them."

Carol stroked her son's head. "Who was it? What did they say?"

He retreated from his mom and sat crouched between both parents. "I don't know. It was some kid ... a girl, I think."

Carol wrapped an arm around him. "What did she say?"

Clark looked up at her. A single tear tracked down his cheek. "*I'm lost. Clark, come help me.*"

Brad looked askance. "You sure?"

The young boy shook his head decisively. "I heard her speak. *'I'm lost. Clark, come help me.'*"

—

The following morning provided little time to discuss the prior night's unsettling events. School day mornings were a bustle of activity, necessary to ensure a timely departure. By 7:15 a.m., the kids were buckled in the SUV, and Brad hurried to drop them off before heading to work.

Carol was alone at the house. The bright sunlight streaming into the country kitchen helped soften the memory of the night before, but Carol couldn't stop thinking about the little girl's plea her son had voiced. She found it downright scary. *Was that what Anne meant about her boys hearing voices in that room?* she wondered, making a mental note to talk with Anne soon.

Carol wasn't a skeptic where the supernatural was concerned and had always accepted it as part of life. Believing in the supernatural was almost akin to believing biblical scriptures. In her mind, there was little difference.

It wasn't that she was prone to experiencing supernatural phenomena, even though she and her cousin, Marie, had always thought the big house her aunt and uncle inhabited was haunted. It was filled with unexplained noises and shadows. But then, it *was* an old house. Carol's only real paranormal experience had occurred years ago at a friend's house one fall afternoon. She and Ginny had been doing homework at the big kitchen table when Ginny excused herself to use the bathroom. Alone, Carol had glanced upward at a sudden sound. A man in a nondescript brown suit stood in the room with her, one foot resting atop a kitchen chair as he worked at tying a shoe. Carol had stared curiously at the stranger until he suddenly returned her gaze, at which point he'd simply disappeared. The vision had left her shaken, but she'd accepted it for what it was.

Had Clark's experience really been any different? she pondered.

Carol spent the rest of the morning busying herself with household chores. Still attuned to the prior night's disturbance, she frequently paused in her work in an effort to assess her surroundings. There was nothing unusual. Even the window above the sink remained closed. Finally, remembering what Anne had said, she decided to investigate the attic, unsure of what she might find but nonetheless feeling compelled to find out.

The crooked little stair to the attic was wedged between the walls separating the rear wing from the main body of the house. The narrow door squeaked loudly as Carol opened it. She paused and looked upward. Instead of darkness, the space seemed flooded with light as the attic, like most Victorian homes, boasted several windows and dormers.

Carol crept up the winding stair, carefully holding on to the rope that served as a makeshift banister. Upon reaching the top, she stood and looked around the lofty space. There was no dirt, no cobwebs. The Guthries had left the house spotless. A few boxes, many of them Christmas decorations, were the vestige of the Maitlands' move, but the bulk of the space was empty.

"Is … is anyone here?" Carol hesitated. She felt a bit foolish. "My name is Carol Maitland. My family and I live here now."

There was no response.

"I'd like to talk to you. Can you hear me?"

Silence greeted her question. Carol sighed and sat on the top step of the attic stair. She didn't hear or see anything. Most importantly, she didn't feel anything. There was no sense of a presence other than the dust motes that drifted lazily in the beams of sunlight. If the beleaguered family members were there, they had nothing to say to Carol. With a sigh, she stood and retraced her steps down the stairway.

———

For weeks, life continued apace. There were a few unexplained noises. The kitchen window repeated its antics from time to time, Maggie continued to police the stairway, and Brad admitted to having experienced the smell of lavender in his office on several more occasions. Clark had abandoned the big bedroom at the end of the hall and taken residence in the guest room closest to his parents' bedroom.

Beyond that, life was almost normal.

Over tea, Carol asked Anne Guthrie about the voices in her sons' bedroom.

"Honestly, I can't remember exactly what the voices said," Anne admitted, reluctantly promising to ask the boys the next time she spoke with them.

Carol found little reassurance in the vow and doubted Anne would actually follow through.

—

In the latter half of October, Renee asked a friend over for the night. Julie DeChamp was a sweet girl, and the Maitlands had known her and her family for years. With Renee occupying the first-floor master suite, Carol and Brad felt certain the teens could make a ruckus without disturbing the rest of the family. Carol provided sodas and snacks and left them to watch Renee's TV before climbing the stairs to bed.

At eleven o'clock, all was quiet.

—

"Dad!" Renee cried out.

Brad woke with a start and struggled to disentangle himself from the bed covers.

"Dad! Dad, wake up!"

Brad quickly sat up, pushed the hair from his eyes, and switched on the nightstand lamp. Renee's face was awash with fear. Behind her, Julie stood at the doorway of the bedroom.

"What's wrong, Renee?"

"You need to get up. The police will be here in a few minutes."

"The police?" Confusion clouded Brad's mind.

Renee nodded vigorously. "I just phoned them. They'll be here soon. Get up!"

Carol roused as her husband stepped out of the bed they shared. "What's going on?"

Still groggy, Brad shook his head. "I don't know."

"There's someone in the house," Renee explained. "I've phoned the police."

Both parents grabbed robes and followed the two girls downstairs. Neither could make any sense of what their daughter was trying to tell them until they entered the foyer.

Renee stopped midway through the space and pointed. "See?"

The door to Renee's suite opened directly off the foyer at a right angle to the front door. To the right of her door had stood two objects: a heavy marble pedestal that displayed a large, ornate oriental vase, and a Chippendale side chair. Neither was there now. The pedestal lay on its side against the closed front door, the vase resting comfortably on the carpet under the grand piano. The Chippendale chair was wedged upside down between the base of the pedestal and the grandfather clock that stood to the right of the entry door.

Brad stood, dumbfounded, and scratched his head. "Good God! What happened?"

Carol wrapped an arm around Renee's shoulders. "Are you girls okay?"

Both girls nodded solemnly.

"Renee, what happened?" Brad asked, his voice anxious.

A weak smile crossed Renee's face. "I don't know. We were watching a scary movie on TV when we began hearing sounds out here. I locked my door, and we tried to hear what was going on. The sounds grew louder, and then there was a big crash. I guess that was the pedestal. Or the chair. I don't know. That's when I called the police." She turned and wrapped her arms around her dad's waist. "I'm sorry, Daddy."

"Nothing to be sorry about. You did the right thing."

Flashing blue and red lights suddenly filled the driveway as a squad car pulled to a stop.

Maggie awoke, her howl adding to the confusion. Order was quickly restored, and the officers entered the house. Renee and Julie did their best to explain what had happened. The officers appeared to take the girls seriously but after checking everything inside and outside, they found no sign of forced entry or exit. There simply were no clues as to what had actually occurred. Clark awoke in the midst of everything and was brought up to speed.

Nearly an hour after they arrived, the officers took their leave. They instructed the Maitlands to phone again should anything further happen.

—

"Exactly what the hell do you think you're doing?" Brad stood staring down at Renee and Julie.

It was early November, nearly one month since the foyer incident. The two girls were seated in the center of the living room, a weathered Ouija board spread out between them.

101

"You know better than to mess with something like that!"

Renee and Julie sat back, quickly leaving the triangular planchette in the middle of the spirit board. They said nothing.

"Where did you get that thing?"

"It's Julie's." Renee blushed.

"Well, get it out of here."

"I'm sorry, Daddy. We were just trying to help."

Brad shook his head in exasperation. "How do you expect this might help?"

Renee swallowed and took a deep breath. "We thought that if we could contact them, we could get them to move on ... leave us alone."

"Where did you get that idea?"

"It's in a book I was reading," Renee admitted.

Brad sighed. "I'm sorry I snapped, kids. Spirit boards ... Ouijas ... shouldn't be taken lightly. I've read about these things, too. Doorways to other realms. Fourth dimensions. As unlikely as it is, if you should happen to open a portal, there's no telling who or what might step through. Just pack it up, okay?"

The girls looked at one another in embarrassment. Julie folded the board and returned it to its box. The planchette followed.

———

Thanksgiving passed quickly, and the Christmas season lay ahead. The Maitlands erected their usual artificial tree in the front living room. The tall tree filled most of the bay window that looked out over the side yard. With the holidays approaching, the family would be spending more time in the living room than in the big, country kitchen.

Around them, the old house seemed to settle and sigh. Carol noticed it immediately. There was a marked sadness she had not sensed before. It was coupled with an unusual sense of tension that, likewise, had not previously been present. Carol felt as if the house was waiting for something to happen. She disliked this sudden change.

Inexplicably, most of the previous activities ceased. The usual noises, the scent of lavender, and the occasional scraping in the attic all stopped. The kitchen window remained closed. Yet these abnormalities were replaced by loud thumps of moving furniture punctuated by an occasional guttural snarl. Both were equally disturbing.

Carol made several pilgrimages to the attic but had no luck in communicating with the previous residents. She began to wonder if they were still there. *If they aren't,* she wondered, *then what is causing the new flurry of activity?* She grew increasingly uncomfortable but tried to hide her feelings from the rest of the family. Ironically, neither Brad nor the children seemed tuned in to what was happening. Was this burden simply hers to bear? She hoped not.

Christmas Eve marked the culmination of weeks of planning, shopping, and baking. Everyone was in a festive mood as they gathered in front of the living room fireplace with hot chocolate and treats in anticipation of Christmas Day. Brad had built a picture-perfect fire in the big marble hearth. Christmas songs from the stereo filled the air.

As the blaze began to wane, Brad rose from his seat next to the fireplace and grabbed the heavy brass poker. "I'll give it a good stir and add another log."

"Wait, Dad." Clark reached for the old Polaroid on the table next to him. "I want to take a couple of photos."

Brad looked at his son and smiled. "Still messing with that old instant camera?"

Clark grinned. "Yes, sir." He moved into position and steadied the camera until he had a good side shot of his father.

Brad stoked the remains of the fire and then reached for a log from the wood basket. He carefully held the log above the brightly burning coals and then let it drop into the flames. A sudden burst of fire filled the fireplace opening and stretched out over the marble hearth. Brad jumped back just as Clark took the photo.

"Jesus! That was close." Brad wiped his forehead. "Almost got me."

Carol laughed nervously. "Be careful. We don't want to burn down the house."

Brad smiled at his wife. "Not to worry. Just got out of hand for a minute."

"Dad. Take a look at this." Clark handed his father the photo, which was now fully developed. Brad stared at the photograph as the color drained from his face.

Carol noticed her husband's reaction. "What is it, Brad?"

"Holy shit," Brad whispered. "What the hell is that?" Reluctantly, he handed the photo to Carol.

Renee joined her mother on the sofa and stared at the photograph. Neither spoke, but a sharp sense of dread crept down Carol's spine.

The photograph was clear and sharply defined. The colors were bright and in stark contrast to one another. Brad was shown falling back from the outpouring of fire, but it was the image within the flames that dominated the scene. It bore a face, one that none of them had ever seen before. An evil visage with eyes no more than deep black holes amidst vivid shades of red and orange. The forehead was high and smooth, the nose long and twisted. But it was the gaping maw of the mouth that was truly terrifying. Lips pulled back in a horrifying grin framed a black, bottomless void that surrounded a disturbingly long tongue.

Clark looked over his mother's shoulder at the photo. "Cool, huh?"

Renee grabbed the photo from her mother's hand and sprang from the sofa. "Hey! Wait! That's mine!"

Clark reached out to intercept his sibling.

Renee flung the photo across the room toward the fireplace, but Clark intercepted it in midflight.

"No way!" He stuffed the photo into his shirt pocket.

Renee lunged at him. "It's evil! It needs to be destroyed!"

At that moment, Maggie lifted her head and began to howl. Her deafening cries filled the living room.

Brad grabbed his daughter's shoulders and separated her from Clark. "That's quite enough! It's just a picture."

Renee wrapped her arms around her father's waist and cried. "It's evil. I know it is. Julie and I must have let something through when we messed with that spirit board."

Holding her close, Brad stroked Renee's hair and stared at Carol solemnly. "No, honey, that's not true. It's only a photo taken with an old camera. Light must be leaking into it, or there's a defect in the film. It's nothing more than that."

Clark crossed his arms in defiance. "I think it's cool."

Carol looked up at her husband, knowing that he considered the visage to be anything but "cool," and she agreed. This was an evil presence, something that had no business being in their home. But how had it gained access to her family? And why? Although Carol had no answers, she now understood what was responsible for the recent supernatural activities. Despite this, she had no idea how to get rid of it.

—

With the exception of the Christmas Eve drama, the holiday passed quickly and quietly. Little was said about what had transpired on that hallowed night, and there was no noticeable activity for the remainder of the year.

Everything changed in January. Doors slammed in the middle of the night, awakening the family and soliciting mournful howls from Maggie. Furniture bumped and slid and was followed by a deep growling. On three occasions, the Maitlands were awakened when every smoke detector in the house chimed in unison. Brad soon disabled each device.

Every night, Clark locked his bedroom door and slid a chest in front of it to discourage any entry. Renee abandoned her room and began sleeping on the chaise lounge at the foot of her parents' bed. The arrangement was far from perfect, but no one complained. It felt better to be close together.

As the unexplainable activities escalated, Carol and Brad considered their options. Neither of them had any real answers.

"What about an exorcism?" Carol suggested, reluctantly.

"That seems too extreme. Besides, we're not even Catholic."

"We could sell."

Brad considered the idea. "It's possible. But if we work with a realtor, assuming we could find one, we'll be obligated to disclose the haunting to potential buyers. I doubt we'd be able to sell anywhere close to market value. We can't afford that kind of financial hit."

They were at an impasse.

As January neared its end, Brad and Carol were still no closer to a solution. At times, the activity would cease for two or three days. During those quiet periods, the Maitlands felt hopeful that the haunting was over, but then the disturbances would begin anew.

Despite the Maitlands' new inhabitant, the presence of the ghostly family could still be felt, but their appearances dwindled. Maggie still studied the open stairway from time to time. The kitchen window occasionally opened. Brad periodically smelled lavender in his office.

Beyond these occurrences, the ethereal family's presence was fairly benign. It was the demon who wreaked havoc.

—

Brad and the kids were off to work and school. Alone with Maggie, Carol stood staring out the kitchen window at the yard beyond. The morning was quiet, but Carol was filled with dread. *If only there was something to be done,* she thought, *some answer to removing this spirit from our home.*

Carol's reverie was suddenly interrupted by Maggie's mournful howl. It came from the second floor and was followed by a distressed yelp as the hound barreled down the stairwell.

"What is it, girl?" Carol met the dog midway through the great room.

Maggie quickly leaped onto the sofa and laid her head against the arm. The whining continued.

Carol sat on the edge of the couch and rubbed Maggie's back. "What's wrong? You okay?"

The crying finally ceased. Maggie looked over her shoulder at her mistress and sighed deeply.

"Something scare you?" Carol asked, only then noticing traces of blood on the dog's pads.

She held one of Maggie's hind legs and examined the foot. It was bloody, but there was no sign of injury. The same was true of the other hind foot. Carol reached for the front paws, but Maggie was having none of it. She curled both feet under her and laid her head back on the sofa's arm.

"Are you hurt?"

Maggie closed her eyes and feigned sleep.

Carol gazed across the room toward the stairway. Somehow she had missed the bloody paw prints that tracked down the steps and across the room. Something was very wrong, and that something was upstairs. Gathering her strength, Carol rose from the couch and gave the old dog a reassuring pat on the head. "You stay here. I'll be right back."

The blood had soaked into the stair runner, leaving a distinct indication of Maggie's journey.

Carol did her best to avoid the stains as she ascended the steps. She reached the second floor, where the trail continued along the railed gallery to the master bedroom. The door was closed. Carol stopped and gasped. On the door's surface, an inverted cross bled brightly. The crimson liquid formed a large puddle on the floor beneath the entrance. Carol finally found the strength to scream.

—

The shock of her discovery had dissipated enough for Carol to turn from the scene and flee down the stairs. *What do I do? What does it mean?* She realized the ominous message was clear: her family was in danger. Questions raced through her mind. *How do I handle this? What can I do?*

First, she had to clean up the blood before Brad and the kids returned home. The thought of such a ghastly task made Carol shiver. How could she possibly stand to touch it?

She walked through the kitchen, past the powder room, and opened the door to the utility room at the end of the short hallway. There, she assembled all she felt she needed for her task: mop, bucket, scrub brush, wipes, and disinfectant. Could she do this? She could think of no other option.

Loaded with her supplies, Carol traversed the hallway again and entered the kitchen. She set the bucket in the sink and began filling it with water. When it was three-quarters full, she lifted the bucket and carried it around the end of the kitchen island. It was then that Carol realized the paw prints were gone. The wood floor shown with its usual mellow tones. *Impossible,* Carol thought. *I'd seen them.*

Setting down the bucket, she knelt beside Maggie and examined her pads. Nothing save the usual roughness from years of walking and running. The dog had fallen into one of her deep sleeps, head still resting on the arm of the sofa.

Carol rose and walked to the foot of the stairs. Ahead of her, the stair runner showed no signs of the bloodstains she'd seen previously. Cautiously, she climbed the steps but found no bloody paw prints along the gallery. Similarly, the floor at the entranceway to the master bedroom was devoid of blood. There was no inverted crucifix to be found. The door stood open, its pristine white panels reflecting the sunlight that flooded the bedroom.

Her body shook nervously. Had she imagined it all? Had the hauntings finally pushed her over the edge? She considered telling Brad about the event but decided against it. She had no proof to offer. Carol was beginning to question her sanity. The last thing she wanted was for Brad to question it as well.

—

The following Wednesday, alone again with Maggie, Carol felt drawn to the attic. She hadn't been up there since packing away the Christmas decorations, and she really didn't understand the sudden need to climb the crooked little stairway.

The day was overcast. When Carol opened the narrow door, she could see that most of the attic was in shadow. She felt for the light switch and illuminated the one spare bulb at the head of the stairs. She gripped the hand rope and slowly ascended the narrow steps. When she reached the top, she saw that the lone light bulb had done little to dispel the gloom. Deep shadows inhabited the tall gables and corners of the vast space.

Carol took a deep breath and slowly sat on the top step. "Hello? Are you here?"

There was no answer.

"I need your help." She suddenly felt like crying. "Can … can you help me?"

Nothing moved, not a sound was uttered. Carol looked around, but there was nothing or no one to be seen. With a stifled sob, she bowed her head. "Please, please help me."

Silence engulfed the room for several minutes when suddenly, Carol caught the faint aroma of lavender. A gentle hand was laid upon her shoulder. Carol felt the slightest breath against her cheek before the whispering began.

———

Several days had passed since her experience in the attic, but now Carol felt she was ready.

Armed with a new resolve, Carol prepared for what she had been instructed to do. Again she was alone with Maggie. Carol had spent the morning hours packing various items she deemed to be vital into the trunk of her car: business papers, treasured photographs, jewelry. She had to be careful not to overdo it. It wasn't easy, but somehow she managed.

Carol looked around the big country kitchen and then turned to the window above the sink and eased it open. The cold breeze felt calming. She would have to remember to close the window later, but, for now, she felt better with it open. Not much else needed her attention.

She walked toward the front of the house and entered the big, formal dining room on the far side of the open stairway. The chandelier above the table was not electrified but was, instead, illuminated by three tiers of candles, eighteen in all. Carol removed the box of matches from her pocket and climbed up onto the table. Starting at the top, she carefully lit each candle. When she had finished, she climbed down and left the room, making sure the door to the foyer was also open.

Once in the kitchen, Carol turned to the gas cooktop. This was the most difficult part of her assignment. She took a deep breath and slowly rotated the knob controlling the largest burner until she could hear the soft hiss of escaping natural gas.

At that moment, the window above the sink slammed shut. Carol simultaneously jumped and screamed. She watched as the window lock slid slowly into place. She had seen the window open many times, but never had she seen it close by itself. Carol stared at the window and forced a smile. "You're going to make sure of it, aren't you?" Her question was answered by a faint scent of lavender that encircled her. It faded and was soon replaced by the sudden odor of rotten eggs and sulfur, a byproduct of the mercaptan additive within the gas.

Carol grabbed her purse and Maggie's leash and crossed to the sofa where the hound lay sleeping.

"Come on, Old Girl. It's time for us to go."

He knew where she was

Jeffrey D. Keeten

He knew where she was.

Hal drove through the night. Through the fog, hounded by his own inharmonious thoughts. He pressed his tired eyes with his fingers trying to induce tears, some moisture to alleviate the grit. A truck roared at him through the fog. Startled, Hal squeezed the steering wheel, feeling the sluggish thump of his discordant heart, as the hurtling shape passed, flinging wind-whipped fog spit across the windshield. The truck's haloed headlights splashed Hal's retinas like sunbursts, blinding him for the space of five anxious blinks.

He heard John Lee Hooker's "Boom Boom" in his ears.

Why was he so afraid of dying?

Hal squeezed his eyes shut and slapped himself hard across the face, bringing tears. Self-pity tears, not tears of pain. They embarrassed him. Made him grit his teeth in frustration. Hal heard his mother's rasp … *Be a man.* He slapped himself again, but this time he was ready for it and turned his head with the slap, like a milksop. *Take it. Take it like a man*, his mother screamed at him.

Hal wanted to slap himself again, but he couldn't raise a hand. He looked at the dark hairs that curled like dead worms against the sweaty skin of his fish-belly hands. Hal felt the burn of his ... *her* ... fingerprints smoldering on his face.

Hal yelled at the windshield, but it was a whimper, not the bellow he needed to hear.

He was pushing it even driving fifty. He cursed the fog. He wanted to drive eighty, a hundred. He wanted to tear a ragged hole in the night. He wanted to displace the darkness like a wraith. He wanted the night to curl away from him like a sliver of sirloin sliced by a bloodstained knife. He wanted the whole world to feel his indignation.

This wasn't how things were supposed to be.

He wanted everyone to know, as a fresh crop of tears sprang to his eyes, that he wanted to kill them all.

Hal hung a left but took the turn too fast and clipped his father-in-law's precious John Deere tractor-shaped mailbox. It raked along the side of his car, screeching like his father-in-law's death-grown fingernails reaching out from the grave. Hal laughed like a giddy child, a sound maniacally mixed with the scraping of paint and the screeching of scratched steel. It was exhilarating and scary. He placed a hand over his mouth to quell the laughter just as his Taurus ran across a deep pothole. The sudden bump caused Hal's hand to involuntarily shove painfully against his nose, eliciting more tears.

It was a night for tears.

The Taurus eased out of the pothole and winced as the undercarriage scraped over the lip of the far side. It irritated Hal. Who was taking care of this road anyway? Something ripped loose from underneath, and suddenly the engine sounded much louder. The vehicle roared down the driveway. Hal dodged some of the potholes and plunged recklessly through others. He could see her black

Mercedes with her childhood swing set curled around as if in a lover's embrace. She'd rammed the trunk of the big elm in the front yard. The Mercedes's hood was crumpled, and behind the cracked tinted windshield, deployed airbags appeared like twin ghostly shadows.

Hal parked and stepped out, greeted by the symphony of cicadas. The winged violins of nature, his uncle used to call them. The Mercedes's door hung open. A black, high-heeled shoe lay on the grass, looking oddly sexy, but lost without purpose. Hal gazed inside the vehicle. The contents of her purse lay scattered like debris from a storm across the floorboard. Her jacket was flung in the backseat, the sleeves twisted like broken appendages.

The fog had lifted some, and Hal could see the dark, twisted form of the battered limbs of the elm against the sky. A chunk of bark, curled in the shape of a boat, had been dislodged by the impact and lay in the adjacent weeds. The house behind the tree sat like a gray figure with slumped shoulders, as if it had been defeated by the elements. Missing shingles created a checkerboard design in the roof. Chips of paint, stripped off the boards by the relentless weather, lay like confetti at the base of the house. A few window panes were shattered, leaving jagged knife-like pieces that sat like splintered teeth in the broken frames. The porch had collapsed.

Hal stopped for a moment to contemplate the destruction, alarmed that so much had happened so quickly. They had buried her mother only two years ago this spring.

The door hung open.

Suddenly unsure, Hal dug both hands deep into his jean pockets. It wasn't how he'd imagined it. In his mind, he'd seen himself walking up the steps to the door and having to force it with a shoulder. He'd never forced open a door and didn't know if it was easy like in the movies, but he felt disappointed that he wouldn't find out. Squinting his eyes, Hal tried to see beyond the dark.

The void within looked as deep as infinity.

Hal took a deep breath and coughed it back out. The air was redolent with the nose-twitching smell of moist cow shit. His father-in-law, facial skin red and crusty with growing cancer, had always laughed when he'd seen him grimace at the smell. He'd clap him on the shoulder and say the same thing every time: "That, my boy, is the smell of money."

Hal walked back to his car and thought to himself, *My daughter needs me.* Not for long.

He picked up the heavy black flashlight from the front seat and the .38 special. Both had belonged to his father, the cop, the hero. The man had been buried with his honors for the past three decades, wrapped in a flag to hold the pieces together. His mother had been in the nursing home for the last seven years. The synapses of her brain were corroded, fried, smothered. She no longer recognized her son, and the relief of being anonymous in her eyes was a tremendous comfort to Hal. He could feel himself growing in her presence. From the dwarf his mother had fashioned, he had steadily been shedding his skin to become something more like himself. It wasn't that easy; the tormentor gone does not completely eradicate the disfigurement from the torments.

Hal shuffled his way up to the house, slipping on wet leaves, only stopping to push aside a column from the porch that had fallen across the path. The wind gusted, and a sheet of droplets fell from the roof, drumming like Philly Joe Jones on his slicker. One of the steps was broken. He jumped the stairs to the landing and heard a board crack beneath his boot. He leaped forward into the darkness.

For several moments, Hal stood in the foyer and listened to the house. It was silent but for the sound of his own breathing. He held his breath and felt the thundering of his pulse in his ears.

He moved the flashlight around and nearly leaped out of his skin when a large piece of wallpaper fluttered down like the wings of a moth. It raised dust that, for a moment, made the scene before him look heavily pixelated. Hal waved his hand, holding the gun ineffectually through the air, but swirling the dust only made things worse. Ghostly shapes of sheet-covered furniture became visible. He flashed the light up the stairway. That's where he needed to go.

Hal's flashlight caught the imprint of her feet, size six, naked. She must have ditched the other shoe somewhere. He squatted to stare at the pretty impressions of her feet in the dust. He felt like Robinson Crusoe looking with amazement at the sand where footprints had never appeared before. He flashed the light up the stairs again. His hunch had been right.

The carpet on the stairs was gnawed. A rat lay on its back on the fifth step, rigid feet flared in the air. Someone must have laid out poison. He nudged the creature. Its desiccated carcass crackled as it tumbled down the stairs.

His mother's voice filled the stairwell. *That girl is too good for you. She could have anyone. In what universe would she ever pick you?* Hal attempted to deflect the echo of her duplicitous words, but they burrowed beneath his skin, casting a cloud of doubt that made his hands tremble. Mother was a master at poisoning the well of his mind, each word a dagger reeking with venom. She was a ghost deep in his psyche, a raspy whisper of rattling chains and shuffling feet.

As Hal ascended the stairs, his anxiety level began to rise. Spiderwebs brushed his face on the landing. It made his skin crawl. He peeled away the cobwebs and rubbed his fingers across his jeans until he could no longer feel the webs' presence. There were more cobwebs ahead, and Hal ducked down to avoid them in a hobbled stance that resembled his late grandmother near the end of her life. He flashed the light ahead but saw nothing but more peeling wallpaper and a crooked colorized photograph of the patriarch of the family, eyes glaring out of the photo and smiling tightly, mouth a red slash of blood. Hal shivered and turned the light away.

Becky had wanted nothing from the house. Not a single memento. The house was an eerie time capsule of the life of a very unhappy family.

At the top of the stairs, Hal flashed the light down the hallway. A rose-colored vase that had once rested atop a narrow table in a nook now lay shattered on the floor. Red shards glittered against the flashlight's rays.

Hal called out her name, too softly, too tentatively. He felt like a boy in church. He batted away more cobwebs. A thud erupted somewhere within the house, and Hal felt the hairs on the nape of his neck rise. He slid against the wall, desperate to blend in with the shadows. Darkness enveloped Hal like a heavy, pungent blanket as he killed the flashlight. He felt large and bulky, vulnerable, like a duelist who had already fired his bullet and could only wait for the discharge of his opponent's weapon.

He stood for what felt like minutes, but was probably only seconds, listening to the subtle language of the house. The creaks, the taps, the unknowable. None of the sounds, he realized, could be attributed to her. Nothing human, nothing alive, but perhaps she was dead. Perhaps she'd killed herself. The thought was a spinning nickel with lots of movement, but it ultimately lost momentum and stalled.

He didn't believe it. He would have to contend with her.

Hal switched the flashlight on, half expecting Becky to be standing before him, posed like Norman Bates with a pair of scissors raised over her head. Ready to paint the walls with his blood. But there was nothing save the vapor trail of the figments of his imagination.

He knew where she'd be.

Hal walked down the hallway, feeling his way along the wall as if he were on a listing ship. He stepped over the broken glass and the table. The pieces of glass crunched beneath his boots. He could only see the prints of her toes as she'd tiptoed by her parents' door, as if they were still slumbering there. He flashed the light into the master bedroom. The trellised rose wallpaper was relatively intact. Several pictures had crashed to the floor, leaving a slightly brighter imprint on the wall where they once hung. Spiderwebs cascaded like highwires for fleas between the posts of the walnut rice bed. The dust on the hardwood floor was undisturbed. A water stain the color of coffee and the size of a manhole cover disfigured the ceiling over the bed. Hal flashed the light on the pale yellow quilt and stared at the brown stains that defaced the cloth in a tie-dye pattern. The smell of must and mold added more flavor to the permeating scent of dust. Hal's nose twitched, and he sneezed.

Something shuffled from a room down the hall; a person, a rat, or some specter his imagination was too stunted to conjure.

Becky's footprints continued down the hallway. She was walking like a model, like a girl still wearing high-heeled shoes. Before sex had become obligatory and methodical, her high-heeled shoes had been a frequent prop in their escapades. Hal smiled grimly as he felt a stirring in his loins at the memories. His gut flooded with the roiling waters of his emotions … love, lust, jealousy, regret, fear … they all jumbled together and became hate.

His fingers tightened around the gun, and he continued down the hallway, making no effort to be quiet.

He knew where she was.

The door to her sister's room was closed. He half-reached for the handle before shaking his head. He was just looking for a reason to stall. Becky wasn't in there. She would never go in there. He flashed the light down the hallway to an open door. Another dark rectangle in an empty frame that beckoned him forward.

Hal stopped outside the door, trying to decipher any shapes in the room, but he didn't need to see. He remembered where the bed was. He remembered the dresser and her desk. He especially remembered the closet.

The closet that she'd forced her father to make. Becky had told her father if he didn't make the closet for her, she would tell. Hal could still remember when she'd shared that story with him. They were both drunk on cheap vodka, and she'd been laughing at the memory of the haunted look on her father's face. The fear of exposure etched in his face. The large man, made small by a defiant twelve-year-old blackmailer. She'd slurred the words while flipping her hair away from her face with a flick of her head. Her father, after his initial shock, had puffed up like a rooster, she'd said, and had hoarsely whispered that if she was no longer willing, then her sister would be.

Father and daughter had stood there glaring at each other, both bluffing, both knowing they would have to give in if push came to shove. Her father was a pillar of the community who couldn't afford even a hint of scandal. Becky knew she couldn't let him do to her sister what he'd been doing to her.

In the end, her father had built the closet.

And sometimes, when he later came to Becky's room, she would lock herself in there, and he'd know he wasn't welcome that night. Her father would tiptoe away, and she would always listen carefully until he was safely past her sister's door. She'd sit in the closet, shivering, telling stories to herself. Stories of revenge and happy endings.

Hal waved the flashlight around the room. Everything was where it had always been. The closet door was shut. If she'd locked it, he would have to break it down.

He switched off the flashlight and walked across the floor, and reached for the latch but hesitated. He didn't have to do this. He could go be with their daughter and leave Becky here, trapped in her past. He moved his finger forward until it touched the door. He could feel her there. Her cheek pressed against the wood, knowing and not knowing who was out there.

He wasn't himself.

Hal thought about just firing all six bullets through the wood. He wouldn't have to see her. Wouldn't have to see her bleed. Wouldn't have to watch her die. He closed his eyes, and then the door slowly creaked outward, revealing the darkness within. Hal's thumb toyed with the switch on the flashlight, but he didn't want to see her in there, a golem, a drooling ghoul, a weightless phantom. He shoved the .38 down into his pants and reached into the darkness until his fingers found the curly blonde mop of her head.

A moment later, Hal hauled Becky out by her hair.

She growled and slashed at his arm with her claws. He threw her at his feet. She hit the floor with a clatter of elbows and knees, howling like an angry spider monkey, and then went silent. She rolled over onto her back. He flicked the flashlight on and squinted at her, not sure what face Becky would reveal. Fear masked his anger. He wanted to kick her. He wanted to kiss her. Her face transformed from placid indifference to feral and calculating. She spread her legs lewdly and winked lasciviously at him. Hal saw a flash of her pale pink panties before knocking her legs back together with a hand. He quickly stepped over Becky, pulled the gun from his pants, and sat down on her chest. She wheezed at the pressure and grinned weakly up at him.

He placed the barrel of the .38 against her right eye.

Becky didn't even blink. The green orb of her eye with the half-moon of blue steel reflected in it continued to stare at him. Both pupils were dime-sized, despite the light. She was spotlighted. A bug flying into a zapper. Becky's lips parted and, for just a moment, Hal thought she was going to speak. Instead, her pink tongue tinged with purple licked her lips.

"Why?" he asked.

Becky tried to spit at him. Her mouth was too dry, and she only managed to spray his hand with a fine mist of saliva. "You know why."

Hal shook his head, resisting the urge to rake the pistol across her face.

"I saw the way you were looking at our daughter. I saved her. Saved her from you." The rasp of her voice was so much like his mother's he almost squeezed the trigger. Hal's stomach flip-flopped. He pulled the gun away from her eye, afraid he'd shoot her before he found out what he wanted to know, what he needed to know.

"No! You're wrong. I love her."

Becky's eyes glittered, and her mouth twisted into a grimace. "But you love her the wrong way."

Hal shut his eyes and swayed over Becky as he tried to center his thoughts. He heard the sound of tearing cloth and the ping of buttons bouncing on the floor. When he opened his eyes, his fingers were kneading one of her prepubescent breasts. Her vivid pink nipple glowed almost transcendentally as it crinkled beneath the calloused grasping of his fingers. The .38 lay on the floor.

"Oh, Daddy, no," Becky said in a small voice. Then her voice changed, becoming that of the sultry nightclub jazz singer that Hal had always loved best of her varied personalities. "Let me see it," she said as she fumbled at his belt and zipper. In the voice of his mother, Becky asked him, "Is she dead?"

The three voices were frolicking around his mind like the witches in *Macbeth*. A simmering pot of confusion.

Hal shook his head. "They said she lost too much blood," he said

122

mournfully. He'd returned from work to find his daughter lying on the kitchen floor in a pool of blood, a butcher knife lodged in her neck. His precious child had stared somewhere beyond him, making guppy fish movements with her mouth. He'd picked her up and rushed her to the hospital. The doctor had told him he'd given her a chance by not extracting the knife. Hal closed his eyes again, playing the desperate scene against the blank screen of his eyelids. When he reopened them, Becky was holding the .38 in one hand and his dick in the other.

"I saved my sister, too," she said.

Hal blinked several times, trying to remember when he'd given her the gun.

"You always said that was an accident," he said.

Becky laughed harshly. "I saved her from him. Exactly like I saved our daughter from you." Becky's voice became his mother's rasp again. "When is someone going to save me?"

"Mother?"

Becky's face twitched. She released her grip on his cock and grabbed his throat. She started squeezing, and Hal was transported back to the Missouri shanty with his mother. Becky's eyes were bulging just like his mother's, her fingers digging deep into his throat, her rasping voice leaving metal filings in his ears that burned hot trails deep into his brain. He tore Becky's hand free from his throat.

"I'm not your mother!" she screamed.

"I'm not your father!" Hal screamed back.

Becky lay her head back down and looked at Hal with bemusement. In the quiet that followed, he thought the screams had broken the spell of their discord. And then she shot him. The report was deafening. Hal felt the impact of the piercing metal burrowing through his skin, puncturing organs, and then exiting out his back to bury itself in the plaster wall behind him. He groaned and toppled off Becky. He felt an inner pressure and the first hot glow of pain.

Becky scrambled to her feet. Hal reached out, wrapping a hairy knuckled hand around her ankle, and she fell to the floor. The gun clattered away from her, sliding along the floorboards and beneath the dresser. It was her turn to groan, and she turned her face, dripping scarlet, toward him.

"You bastard! You fucking bastard!" Becky screamed as she shook off his grip and stumbled to her feet. Hal rolled over and staggered as he, too, rose, surprised that his limbs still worked. He felt both light and cumbersome. Hal shoved his cock back into his pants and zipped up as he lurched toward Becky.

Fear sparked in Becky's eyes, and she turned to flee. Hal's fingers snagged at her blouse, arresting her escape for only a second before the cloth ripped free, leaving him with her shirt as she fled down the hallway naked to the waist. Hal hit the doorway with his shoulder and nearly fell over. His hand grabbed the top of a doorframe, and he managed to steady himself. He heard a clatter as Becky crashed into the hallway table. Becky was rasping, gasping, and cursing. Hal continued his pursuit, blood soaking his clothes.

Hal watched Becky rise to her feet again. A pale shape in the gloom of the hallway. Somehow he still had the flashlight. He became snared with the table as well. He felt like Frankenstein's monster, clumsily thrashing and growling, as he finally freed himself. Ahead, Becky stood at the head of the stairs and grinned at him, her face monstrous in the flickering glow of the flashlight.

"You can't win. You never have, and you never will," Becky rasped from Hal's mother's mouth.

Hal threw the flashlight. It turned over and over, splashing the floor and the ceiling in a kaleidoscope of flickering light. Becky seemed mesmerized by its passage, realizing too late the trajectory until it smashed against her head. She lifted her arms, searching for balance. She reached backward with a foot and stumbled down the long stairway, a coda of cries, and that ended in sudden silence.

The warm blood had turned cold. So much blood, flowing from his beautiful daughter, from Becky's face, from his own mortal wound. All of it streaming downward to squelch in his shoes. Hal shivered and wrapped his arms around himself as he lurched down the seemingly lengthening hallway.

The stairs were difficult. Each step required a complete will of concentration. He stopped at the landing and gazed down at the shape of his wife at the bottom of the stairs. A broken Barbie, sprawled in ways in which only a disarticulated doll should lie. This is where they had found her, Becky's twelve-year-old sister. An "accident."

He stared down as he stepped over her. Becky was a smudge in the darkness. She wasn't his mother. She wasn't herself. She wasn't anything anymore.

Hal nearly fell three times on the way to the car. He knew if he did, he would never get back up. His phone glowed from the cupholder with a missed message. He opened the car door. It felt heavy, like the entrance to an ancient tomb. Something tore inside as he gave the door one last heave. He stood there gasping for air, holding his side, feeling his life leak out of him in a torrent. It took him three excruciating tries to lean over and snag the phone. He stabbed at the button with bloated and clumsy fingers and listened to the recorded message.

"This is Doctor Hector Rodriguez. I'm calling to inform you that surgery was a success. Your daughter is stable. She is resting now, and I expect her to make a full recovery. You were extremely lucky tonight. If you could come to the nurses' station, we have some paperwork for you to fill out."

The phone slipped from Hal's hand. He tried to catch it but only managed to punch it away from himself. It tumbled into the darkness, a thousand miles away. Hal's knees chose that moment to fold up like an accordion. He fell hard to the ground, and the contact knocked the wind out of him. He rolled over onto his back, gasping for air. Everything was black, except for the tiny flashes of lightning flaring at the edges of his vision. Hal expected to hear his mother's voice, but she was mercifully silent. Bringing air into his body was painful, and he didn't want to do it anymore.

He willed it so.

The Urraca Affair

James Goodridge

A bank teller's scream rises above an exchange of gunshots from within the Eastern Bank at Fortieth and Third on a spring afternoon. Three masked men in identical gray flannel suits, brown fedoras, and black scarves concealing the lower halves of their faces, wave gats, daring customers to move. A fourth urban desperado is sprawled out on the floor, a bullet hole ventilating his forehead courtesy of the bank's gray-uniformed guard, now on his knees with a bullet wound to his arm. Eastern Bank's penny-pinching refusal to upgrade in design and security makes it an easy mark in 1931.

Mr. A bellows instructions to his crew, voice deep with a metallic edge. "Mister C, grab up the money bags and hustle them to the cars! Mister D, grab the bank dick! He might come in handy if things go south! Mister B is useless now—leave him!" He turns to face the unfortunate bank customers bearing witness to the burglary. "Down on the floor, boys and girls—now! If you're smart, you'll stay there for the next five minutes! Don't any of youse be a wisenheimer!"

"Please, I've—" Before hoary-mustached guard Wilbert Scanlon can finish pleading for his freedom, Mr. D raps him across the chin with the butt of a .38. "Shaddup, youse!" Mr. D, often sadistic, likes working folks over.

Mr. C and Mr. A walk briskly out the bank doors and hop into a black 1930 Ford sedan. A rubbery-legged Wilbert is pushed by Mr. D into an identically colored Ford van that sports a spinning radar dish on its roof. A fifth criminal, Mr. E, sits behind the wheel as a mysterious figure in the back turns knobs on a radio console. Under the shadow and roar of the Third Avenue El, the getaway cars peel off from the curb with an exquisite haul.

—

My name is Urraca Vouxhall, an occult detective, and this is my tale.

Evening finds me at my desk typing out a new etiquette column for tomorrow's *New York Evening Journal*. When not conveying social dos and don'ts, my other status of employment is subcontract work for my dear friends Madison Cavendish and Seneca Sue, private investigators of the occult, paranormal, and mundane.

"Miss Uvee, you ready for your supper?" It's more a timid demand than a question from my maid, Audrey Standhope, a plump strawberry-blonde-haired woman. She's holding a silver tray with my food and a folded copy of this evening's *Journal*. Draped over one of her arms is my blood-red silk kimono, which, par for the course, matches almost every item in my apartment, which is done up in various shades of red. I adore the color.

Audrey interrupts my cerebral flow. "Wait until you see your employer's headline. Boy howdy, the city's in a crime conniption!"

"What's that you say, Audie?" Advising readers on the proper way to eat raw oysters will have to wait. Unfolding the newspaper next to my plate of sweetbreads, eggs Portuguese-style, raw carrots, and lemon tea, the *Journal's* headline shouts of another bank robbery earlier today over in the Turtle Bay neighborhood of Midtown Manhattan.

Abruptly, the telephone's bell comes to life across the room; before I can look at Audie, she's flicking the phone cord out so I'll be able to answer from my writing desk.

"Hello, Urraca? How ya doin', love?" asks Madison Cavendish in his 33rd-and-Third-Avenue-with-a-dab-of-Harlem-spice accent.

"Evening, dearest. I get the feeling the pace of my evening is going to pick up. What's the affair?" Pointing to the kimono, I shoo it and Audie away, sticking with my crème-red blouse, black slacks, midnight pearls, and pumps. This call is going to interrupt my viola-playing regimen after dinner, I figure.

"I need your assistance. Have you perused the front page of your paper yet?"

"I see a bank robbery. But what's that got to do with the occult?" I poke a little sweetbread up with my fork to answer the hunger pull of my stomach.

"More like what's it gotta do with *you*," Madison chuckles, which I don't find amusing. Money is tight, but a female John Dillinger I am not. "The Eastern Bank was knocked over by a gang of zombies!" Madison stops chuckling, and I drop my fork. "Part of a string of robberies."

"How do you know this?" I am skeptical; it is just too ludicrous.

"One of the robbers was shot in the head. When detectives arrived at the crime scene, the body had accelerated in decomposition, accordin' to witnesses. The bank guard, Bert Scanlon, was winged and taken hostage. Later he was found in an alley near Leroy Street in the West Village, the top of his head cracked open, and his brain scooped out as if it was a three-minute egg. As usual, when the city's Office of Special Concerns feels a case has too much weird mustard for them, they farm it out to Sue and me, but for this, we would value your help," explains Madison. Sue is Madison's partner/gal/shaman by day, werewolf by night, depending on the moon's nocturnal mood.

"And what do you need me to do, Madison?" If all this is true, it will make for an uncanny affair—the type I crave.

"I need your connections. I need for you to get the skinny on who's behind this," says my quasi boss. You see, I'm the Elsa Maxwell of the occult world and paranormal underground. Creepy gossip mixed with blind items are what I deal in, along with solving enigmatic affairs.

"You know you can count on me. I can't turn you down, dear." I am sincere about that, given our history. I am grateful to them. Had Madison and Sue not come across me—a quivering mess cooped up in a cage due to my diabolical ex-husband Dr. Cranston Vouxhall's alchemist experiments—I would have languished away in Cranston's lab forever and a day, on Welfare Island, back in 1921. To this day, I get antsy at the sight of cages or jail cells.

"Fifty percent of the reward is yours. Plus, the Stonenan family has kicked in some money, bein' that Eastern Bank handles the Giants' vendor accounts. It's not a far reach to say, Urraca, that Harry M. Stevens is hot like one of his wieners about this," Madison cracks wise about the Polo Grounds concessionaire. I like his offer.

"Bayonne Benny." His name pops into my head.

"Who?" Madison doesn't know of my connection.

"He's a ghoul that skulks about in Woodlawn Cemetery up in the Bronx. Used to be muscle for Kid Dropper out in Coney Island. Made the mistake of shacking up with a strumpet from the Bronx named Molly, who poisoned him in a fit of green-eyed envy. She got the chair, and he got a huzzah of a funeral.

I'll take the job." Due to the sorrowful economic times we're in, the fortune I made as owner of the Peerless candy and confection company was shaved in half, hence my current employments.

"Okay, Miss Vouxhall. Do what ya do best and get back to me," Madison says, ending the call. Not that I need to, but by doing my best, he means my femme fatale charm. I call Audie out of the kitchen. We've got work to do.

"Oh, for corn's sake, Miss Uvee. You know I hate—and I do mean *hate*—going up to Woodlawn at night!" When not fussing over me and being a total round bundle of nerves, Audie is a first-class folk medicine woman and conjurer adept in powwow from Hex County, Pennsylvania.

"Oh, come on, Audie. You know you'll be splendidly safe," I assure her.

"Well, just in case, I'm going to smudge my body with sage and Saint John's root before we leave, and I'll sit with Melbern at the front gate guardhouse when we get there. Don't want to be around that man."

"Be that as it may, Audie dear, get things ready. We visit Benny after midnight," I say, nibbling on my dinner before it gets too frigid.

———

After dinner, Audie helps me apply flesh-colored theatrical makeup to my face and other exposed areas of my skin. The special makeup that covers up my gray pallor, concocted by an associate of Madison's, Dr. Obelin Pythagoras, makes it possible for me to be out in public for long periods of time, except in arctic cold or desert heat. A transfusion of vampire blood of the cosmic horror variety from Madison back in 1921 christened me a vampire/cognizant zombie hybrid—and, if I may say, laced with a touch of Park Avenue elegance and panache.

"Please be careful, Miss Uvee," whispers Audie while securing our imperial-blue Studebaker near the front gates of Woodlawn, the second-to-last-gates legions of souls inside pass through before going up to the pearly ones or down to the gates of hades.

"Benny's never been a problem before. Sometimes a bit too touchy-feely, but I can handle him." In a fire-engine-red cheongsam dress wrapped in a mink coat, I look delectable, but I have something more delightful for Benny in a pink hatbox secured by a pink bow.

"Well, I'll be Mississippi goddamned! How ya'll be doing? It's been some time, Miss Vouxhall and Miss Audrey." A portly black man dressed in a horizon-blue guard uniform lumbers to the gate and greets us. Melbern St. Henry has a touch of voodoo knowledge and was behind Benny's resurrection to help get Melbern through the lonely graveyard-shift hours.

"Hello, Melbern dear, has Benny been around?" I slip a crisp Lincoln fin into his hand. Melbern quickly retreats into the guard office to examine the bill's authenticity under a lone desk lamp.

After a minute, Melbern returns and opens the gate for us. "Miss Vouxhall, he be at his usual spot, but ornery since I beat the lightning out of him in a few checker games. Benny don't like to lose."

"Well, I've got to see him, dear. Audie's going to keep you company while I go over to his mausoleum. Audie can give you a quick game of checkers while I'm gone." And with that, I leave the two of them to walk into the darkness of Woodlawn, Audie's voice making a game wager in the distance.

The path to Benny's not-so-final resting place bisects damp grass and headstones, the moisture receiving a burst of a spring breeze that rustles elms and sycamore tree leaves in the witching hour. Every now and then, I feel an infinity pull, as Seneca Sue likes to call it, when the worlds of the living and dead cross from graves of poor souls wanting to gush or moan about their former life and why they haven't entered the final gates. Sorry, I just don't have the time to chitchat.

"Benny?" I whisper into the darkness of his mausoleum. "Oh Bennyyyy?" I say a little louder in a singsong voice.

"Well, well, well! I'll shave a cat if it hasn't been a month of Sundays since you and those gams of yours have been here to visit. I was just about to hop in my box, sweetie!" says Benny. Even though Benny is half dead, he still looks a little dapper in a tattered black suit, its style cut from a decade ago. Icy dead-as-a-halibut blue eyes and hay-golden hair mottled with mossy bald patches of gaunt gray skin shows how much of a step down Benny—a former thug, pimp, gunman, and police informant—has taken in the underworld. Benny has a Jersey accent that could rival Madison's.

I take a seat on top of his casket next to him. "Benny, I'll get straight to the point. I need some dope on a bank robbery."

"You gotta be kiddin', right? Bank jobs are for the livin'." In the light of the moon filtering into his resting place, I see his bony hand moving towards my silk stocking-wrapped thigh and shimmy away.

"Benny, it was knocked off by a gang of zombies. Come on, handsome. You've got to know something." I shouldn't have made that handsome quip.

"Who wants to know?" His bony hand is at it again. I place the hatbox between us; it is a good bulwark.

"I do. The last bank robbed does business with the Giants' front office."

"I'm a Dodgers fan, so good for them." Benny's bones crack as he shrugs.

"Listen, Benny. The powers that be are going to treat me lovely if I help them out on this affair. Any dope you have on the crime will go a long way with me. Here is an incentive…"

I untie the bow and take the lid off the hatbox; Benny stares down at the human brain that resides within.

"Looks yummy, doesn't it?" I bribe. "It's yours if you give me a tip on who's behind these robberies."

"Whose is it?" Although his pallor is gray, Benny's face makes a noncommittal, almost fleshy grimace as though he is looking over the brain in an Essex Street butcher shop. Benny is picky.

"Shark McCoy, a Tenth Avenue thug. I managed to get it through my coroner's connections after the cops riddled him with bullets down on Pitt Street when they walked up on him sticking up a swell. Had it in my fridge for special occasions." I let Benny sample it with a bite.

"Uh…okay, okay. There's a doctor I see named Belmont Langora. Ten years ago, he was big muck in the world of medical research on the brain's five waves after death—not the voodoo stuff our buddy Melbern does nor the alchemist necromancy bunk of your ex-husband. But Langora got caught doin' unauthorized surgery on primates in Brooklyn, so's the AMA sanctioned him but let him keep his shingle, see."

"And what's the connection to the bank jobs?" The cool night air vapors my words, but not Benny's; his are of rot and compost.

"Langora's been makin' the rounds of cemeteries seekin' out zombies or ghouls like me, givin' us a song and dance about electropulse rejuvenation. But he charges a fee, and whoever is short on funds knocks over banks to make the amount to get it," Benny says between squishy bites.

"And his location?" I push the hatbox closer for him to enjoy his thawed-out snack.

"Long Island City, near the railroad tracks behind Bloomingdale's warehouse. Can't miss the house cuz it sticks out in the neighborhood. The front of the joint he uses is an electrical massage parlor caterin' to high-society biddies on the hunt to look young again. Just a money-makin' ruse. Did I ever tell ya I love ya, Urraca?"

Wow. His *I love you* came from left field.

"Let's talk about that some other time. Thanks, Benny." I'm grateful.

"You're welcome, toots!" says Benny, sulking as I leave him to enjoy his after-midnight snack.

Back at the gates, Audie is minus three bucks via Melbern.

—

A phone call and a few starry nights later finds me in front of a sinister-looking house that could have been designed by Franklin Lloyd Wright if I didn't know any better by its modern yet temple-like structure.

"Just park up the block, Audie, and give me a solid hour to snoop and ask questions." I step out of the Imperial in a sunrise-red beret securing flowing midnight hair, wearing a red dress with a silver lizard brooch pinned to it. My gams, as Benny likes to call them, are covered with man-catching black fishnets, and I'm wearing shiny black high heels. A .38 is in my clutch bag at the ready. According to the appointment I made with Dr. Langora, electropulse electrodes attached to my temples will produce a soothing pulse that would give me vitality.

"Hello, Miss Vouxhall. Welcome," says Dr. Langora, ushering me into an azure and gold Egyptian-looking sitting room with plush couches in stalls past it. The doctor, an imposing man in a lab coat with a noticeable black widow's peak, gives off an air of European regalness. "I'm glad you kept your appointment. So sorry to have you come in after hours," says the doctor.

"Oh, doctor, I do hope this helps slow down Father Time for me per our phone conversation," I say in rich dowager character while signing "don't litigate me" release forms, freeing the doctor from negligence.

"Now that the paperwork is signed, my dear, shall we go for a treatment?" Instead of going to a stall, Langora beckons me behind a glass counter stocked with beauty items. One button clicked by Langora locks the shop door, and another click slides a wooden wall panel open. Mysteriously beyond it, primary-colored lights blink, fighting the room's darkness. "Come in, my dear. You're not afraid, are you?"

"Me? No. But it would be divine to see where I'm going." I feel around in my clutch bag to locate the .38. Suddenly, a light switch is flicked on, illuminating the room.

"Benny!" I yell.

Langora wrenches my clutch bag out of my hands.

This is *not* good.

"Benny, you double-crossing heel!" An arrogant shove by Langora has me bumping up against Benny, who plants a foul-breathed kiss on my cheek. Ew!

Sharply dressed in a gaudy tangerine and lime-green pinstripe suit better fit for a sideshow barker, a small, metal pentagram-shaped device is stamped behind Benny's right ear, blinking my favorite color.

"Listen, you! You shouldn't have come by Woodlawn askin' me questions, see!" Benny's voice is now a metallic basso profundo. His grip on my wrists is cold and tight—so tight I can feel the stitches that keep my right hand attached to my body loosen. "A dame like you likes to play with a ghoul's feelings. Well, I'll settle your hash!" thunders Benny.

"Benny, you're hurting me!"

"Shaddup or I'll blacken those pretty blue eyes of yours! Stop strugglin'!

So help me, I'll—"

"Now now, Benjamin. She's needed alive…if that's what she is," chuckles Langora, hefting up my dress sleeve past the theatrical makeup exposing my gray skin. "Compose yourself, my friend. I promise after I'm finished with her, she's all yours." Again with the chuckles. A funny man he is.

"Some of that vampire blood in your veins, I'm told, could work in tandem with my electropulse console. Could be an asset to me," says Langora.

"You mean *us!*" snarls Benny.

I see a double-cross in their future. But right now, I have a bigger problem. Looking around, what I now see is a laboratory, and I get frantic. In a corner is a holding cell…

"So I guess you're going to create a zombie army and take over the world. Am I right?" Gotta be sassy to hide my growing terror.

"Please, I'm in it only for monetary gain," says a smiling Langora.

"If you play ball with me, maybe you can take Mister B's place, aka Lenox Lenny, in the gang or be my gun moll. Whaddya say?" Benny's got feelings, I guess, but …

"I'd rather hang, Benny!" I can't help it. A whack across my mouth draws a trickle of my glowing magenta blood the doctor is so interested in. I feel sorry for Benny because now he's taking it to another level. "You're going to pay for that slap, Benny."

"Lock her in the holding cell! We've got to go over the plans for the Yonkers bank job. We will tend to her later!" commands Langora, to which Benny, with a metal laugh, waltzes me over to the holding cell against my panicking struggles. With a palmed mush to my face, I'm shoved and locked in.

"See ya later, toots!" crows Benny in that sickening voice.

Langora brings the console to life before they head down to the basement. With the door left open, I hear the moans of the living dead morph into lively thug bravado. I scream as the encroaching feel of the steel cell bars starts to affect me.

"Poise, Urraca, poise. You can't go back …" I whisper to calm myself. But my screams turn to zombie moans. Looking down at my right hand, the stitches are loosening to a dangle. I start to mindlessly grab about my body.

"Got…to…be…a…way…out…Urraca."

Then I feel the brooch.

—

Leaning up against the cell bars, I take a deep breath and grapple with the lock using my brooch pin. The voice of Langora rises like a muffled college lecturer from the basement mixed with metallic-edged questions being asked. "Got … it!" I rasp. Slipping out of the cell, I feel my strength flowing back, but my right hand's almost detached.

Standing in front of the console, I have no time to figure out Langora's oscillating monstrosity's control over the gang. Summoning up all that's in me, I lift up a wooden chair with my left hand. I make like Benny's parched leathery face is the console and come down hard on it. The blow throws me, along with a plume of colored sparks, across the room. My right hand rolls around on the floor. The console's eruption is filling the room with choking smoke. Like a cerebral light switched off down in the basement, the gangs revert to their walking-dead selves.

"Back! Back! Stop! I made you! Go no further, I order!" shouts Langora, backing up the basement stairs with the sounds of a horrific struggle. I am frantic to locate my hand so I can get out. Langora's shrill screams cut throughout the lab. Fighting like the devil that he is to avoid the grasp of his former gang is to no avail. Pulled down to the gray lab floor, his former partners in crime commence their feast. Flaying the doctor's hair and skin off, his skull is cracked open to a succulent cerebral cortex. I must say that for a second, I want to join my zombie brethren, but coughing from the acrid black smoke brings me back to the job of getting out. I throw my right hand into my now-singed red clutch bag and start crawling away.

"Hey, toots, where ya goin'?" Benny asks with a shrill otherworldly laugh, yanking me up off the floor.

"You and I will rot in hades, Benny! I … I …" It's the last thing I remember yelling before the smoke overtakes me.

———

The magenta liquid life force coursing through my veins brings me out of the dark void I know all too well.

"You'll be ready to go back to your column and bass fiddle in a few days, love," whispers a pencil-thin mustache to me. Focusing my eyes, I realize the pencil mustache belongs to my quasi boss, Madison Cavendish. He's lying next to me with his sleeve rolled up, a transfusion of his blood into me courtesy of Dr. Pythagoras, who's standing at the edge of the bed I'm in, his brown face a dour mask.

I feel a nudge to my right wrist and look over to see Seneca Sue seated next to the bed, finishing work to reattach my right hand with surgical stitching.

"Yowza, honey! Glad you're back among the living, for what it's worth," says Sue, a mystical sepia beauty.

"Boy howdy to that!" Audie is at the foot of the bed, nervously wringing her hands. After a minute or so of zombie moans, I get my voice and syntax back.

"What happened?" Groggy or not, I have to hear this.

"Well, Miss Uvee, I didn't like you inside that place, so I shaved a few minutes off the wait time you had told me, and good thing I did. I pulled up to that evil place, smoke billowing out. I sent a few .38 slugs into the door to open it up. The panel door was a bit harder, so I hexed it open in time to see that Bayou … Bay … whatever, Benny dragging you to where only the spirits know, while the rest of those undead hoodlums were gnawing on that … that … doctor! But I fixed Benny but good, emptied the rest of my slugs in Benny's head, I did. He won't bother you no more, Miss Uvee!" At hearing this from her, I am surprised at Miss Standhope's grit.

"For Audrey to be a nervous Nellie, she sure has in her some elan," says Sue.

"Thank you, Audie." I mean it. "Now, where am I, and how long have I been here?"

"You're at Madison's apartment on Riverside Drive, and it's been a few days. Audrey felt it was best to bring you here. Everything was touch and go. That's when Madison decided to give you another transfusion," says Dr. Pythagoras, placing some of the tools of his trade back into his black house-call bag. "Audrey's a gem. She's been ghostwriting your column. I submit that you give her a salary increase." I wish the good doctor hadn't said it, but he is right, and I will.

"And?" Everyone is aware of what I want to know.

Sitting up, Madison rolls down his shirt sleeve. "The Office of Special Concerns sent a forensic squad out to Langora's place once the fire department gave the okay. Mostly ashes there. Langora was a piece of chewed-up barbecue.

That mysterious machine is blackened rubble, which makes it hard for us to figure out its function. But we do know that the gang consisted of Leadfoot Fritz, a getaway driver from Yonkers; Lenox Lenny, a gambler from Harlem; Nick the Greek, a yegg from the Lower East Side; and Roy Lamont, a sadistic stickup man from Maryland. All recently deceased. Sorry, youse two...no Bayonne Benny. The graveyard-shift guard up at Woodlawn was found murdered, and Benny's body has vanished."

"Boy howdy," says Audie. Her nervousness is returning. Me, I am more upbeat. If Benny comes back next time, I'll be the one to deal with him, not Audie. I say a silent prayer for Melbern St. Henry.

"Viola," I say.

"What?" Madison looks at me, waiting for the gag line.

"It's a viola, not a bass fiddle," I say. Everyone chuckles, even Dr. Pythagoras.

I know you'll be back, Benny. And I'll be waiting.

"There is magic in the Night when pumpkins glow by Moonlight."

Unknown

All Hallows'

Morgan Golladay

On this night, the souls are loosed.
They wander freely,
seeking a saucer of milk by the door,
an open window,
someone to relay a message,
a blessing, a curse.

This is when we whistle past the graveyard,
and avert our eyes from the lady in white,
the red-eyed specter, the ghostly sheen in the trees.
We try to ignore the whisper at the hearth and
the owl, calling our names in the dark.

Some take refuge at bedside,
or near the altar, or reciting their magic texts.
Palpable fear clutches some hearts;

others cast a blind eye to superstition
while making the sign against the evil eye
behind their backs.
But all feel the thinning of the veil,
the invitation to cross the bounds,
to reach out a hand and touch the unimaginable.

Los Dios de los Muertos
on these Dias de Los Muertos
allow all to wander free,
whether in bardo, purgatory,
Elysian Fields, or Valhalla.
The grieving and the grieved join hands.
But who is to say whose hands are whose?

It Is Highly Illegal to Hit someone with an Egg

Morgan Golladay

It's Fried-day in the 'burb.
My neighbor played loud music
all night.
Called the cops. No response.
I'm afraid to confront them.
They egged my car last Halloween.
That was a mess.
Paint scratched, dent in the hood,
Egg white and yolk stuck like glue
To the windshield vents.
Think they had some hard-boiled attitude.
Not worth the hollandaise sauce
to ask them over to talk—
a soft-boiled approach to
working out our problems.
Somehow things between us got scrambled.

Was it the salsa line
at our last street party?
The roofers (Benedict and Sons)
starting at 7 in the morning?
It wasn't us who poached their tomatoes
In their garden.
But they seem to have it in for us.
The devil seems to have gotten into them,
and has made a real hash of
our neighborly relationship.
And while they are sitting there
with egg on their faces,
I wonder if a custard pie might ease tensions.

The Gravid Doe

Morgan Golladay

She lay still.
Beautiful in her death,
the mourners gathered,
dressed in accustomed black,
waiting for the funeral feast.
Undeterred by passing traffic,
they blessed the bounty,
crowded to the altar,
dipped their beaks
and fed.

My thoughts return
to cycles.
There is a beauty and a rhythm
in this continuing story:
she feeds these vultures,
who, like me,
will eventually feed others.

Devil's Throne

Morgan Golladay

Across the Shenandoah,
over foothills at mountain's base,
you can catch a brief glimpse of the rockfall.
Centuries after the land slipped
on this, my mountain,
rains and winds moved the dirt,
subtly shifting soils and organics,
washing slides and rock faces clean.

All a-tumble,
these mountain bones are bare to the sun,
sheltering only a few hardy brambles
left by passing birds
and a slow-moving tide of stunted trees.
Locals call it Devil's Throne,
for he sat there, contemplating his fall,
and burning all life with his body's fire.

I think of it as a place of solitude,
strength, and sorrow,
home to small ones,
snakes, voles, mice;
a place of absolutes—
predator and prey.

"Demons are like obedient dogs;
they come when they are called."
Remy de Gourmont

Are you Lonesome ToNight?

Bernie Brown

The breakfast dishes clanked as Sally loaded the dishwasher. Her husband Emmet stopped in the kitchen on his way out the door. With an exasperated sigh, he said, "You should load from the back to the front. How long does it take you to learn that?"

Sally's lips pinched tightly together.

He tightened his tie over his bulging neck and looked at her Elvis life-sized cutout with disgust. "That is the stupidest thing." He gave it a kick.

Sally caught Elvis before he toppled over and glared at Emmet's back as he left. She set Elvis upright, brushed imaginary lint from his white jumpsuit, and gently examined where Emmet had kicked him. No damage. A slight smudge. She brushed at it with a cloth, and it came clean. Sally kissed her fingertips and placed the kiss on Elvis's cheek. "*He's* the stupidest thing. I'd like to give him a kick." She then proceeded to load all the dishes at the front of the dishwasher.

The white jumpsuit worn by the Elvis cutout had been one of his costumes at his Hawaii comeback concert. She had been seven in 1973 when the concert was broadcast. His fancy footwork, the dramatics with the microphone, the song "Suspicious Minds" all remained clear in her mind. Most of all, she remembered the scarves he blotted his face with. He had worn several loose around his neck and tossed them to the audience, one at a time, as he used them.

Sally found Elvis at Anything and Everything, a thrift store in the Old Market. Emmet gave her very little money to furnish their house, so Sally knew all the secondhand shops in town. Right there in the middle of Anything and Everything, Elvis had winked at her for the first time. She couldn't be certain if she imagined it or if her empty heart's desperate yearning had made him wink.

That day she brought the cutout home. She bought three thin and silky scarves from the Dollar Store. One yellow, one blue, and one red. She draped them around the cutout's neck. Emmet's kick had sent them flying. With tender care, she stooped to pick each one up.

———

Emmet had already been a blustery, arrogant man when they first met. When a used car dealership offered him a job, he asked her to marry him. Cocky and full of himself, he was sure he'd succeed.

Sally had never loved him—didn't even like him—but he gave her a way out of her stale and joyless life. At both her dad's musty-smelling accounting office and their rundown shabby house, she had tracked the meager finances, cleaned, fixed coffee, answered the phone, and done the shopping.

Emmet's proposal might be the only one she ever got. She took it.

As the years went by, Emmet remained at the bottom of the heap at the used car dealer. He added bitterness, resentment, and bullying to his list of unpleasant characteristics.

Sally stayed because she had nowhere to go except back to her father's office and house.

———

Emmet wanted exactly the same menu on exactly the same night each week. Monday meatloaf, Tuesday tuna casserole, Wednesday beef stew, Thursday hot dogs on buns, Friday cheeseburgers, Saturday pork chops, Sunday fried chicken. Sally wanted to try some of the recipes she saw on the cooking shows, but Emmet would never eat them. Worse, he would berate her for cooking them.

Tonight was meatloaf night, which Sally served with baked potatoes and green beans.

Emmet sat at the table like a king waiting to be served.

Sally thought, *There's a king in this kitchen, but it's not you.* She placed the dishes within easy reach of Emmet, who piled his plate high.

"Last week's meatloaf was more flavorful. And you know I like vegetables well-cooked," he scoffed.

Sally looked at Elvis for sympathy and swore he winked.

Emmet removed himself to the living room, where he turned the television on high volume.

Only half a piece of meatloaf, a shriveled potato, and three green beans were left at meal's end. Sally ate them as she cleared the table.

The television noise drowned out the Elvis Pandora station. She turned up the volume. Emmet turned up the TV volume. Sally turned up the Pandora volume.

The loathsome man came into the kitchen and saw her loading the dishwasher from front to back. "Turn down that blessed noise." He muted her iPhone and shoved her out of the way to reload the dishwasher. "That's how it should be done."

Sally's face burned hot with shame and hatred. She spent the rest of the evening reading in the kitchen, enjoying her privacy and a peanut butter sandwich to fill her unsatisfied stomach.

—

Next morning, Emmet opened the Captain Crunch box and poured cereal into his bowl. Amid the cereal, a bloodstained blue scarf slithered out. "What's this?" He dangled it in front of Sally. "Is this your idea of a joke?" He tossed the scarf in her face.

She pulled the scarf off and backed away. Her hands turned clammy. "I didn't have anything to do with it. I swear." She glanced at the Elvis cutout, noticing that the blue scarf was missing. Again, he appeared to wink at her.

Emmet moved threateningly close. "How did it happen then? You and that stupid cutout. I have a mind to set it on fire." He slammed out the front door, calling over his shoulder, "Get rid of that thing."

—

She leaned against the sink, taking deep breaths to steady herself. She tried to remove the bloodstains from the blue scarf, but her effort failed. Sally folded the scarf, stains and all, and stuck it in the bottom of her underwear drawer.

Elvis stayed in his usual spot until just before Emmet's expected arrival. Then Sally set him in the back closet, the one Emmet never used. It stored luggage and Christmas decorations. She looked Elvis in the eye. "Sorry. I'd rather stick *him* in here. It's just until he leaves for work tomorrow." She straightened his two remaining scarves.

—

When Emmet came in the kitchen for supper, he said, "I see you finally got rid of that stupid cutout. Don't think about replacing it, either."

Sally turned away so he couldn't see the hate in her eyes.

Emmet chomped the tuna casserole with an open mouth. Pieces fell to his shirt. Bits of noodle clung around his mouth. "You should have used more liquid with the mushroom soup. This is dry as dust. And you know I like light tuna, not dark."

"The store was all out of light."

"You should have gone to another store, then."

He left enough casserole that Sally didn't need to supplement with a peanut butter sandwich. She fantasized about putting poison in the beef stew tomorrow night. He'd clutch his throat and tumble over like a sack of feed, retching and foaming at the mouth. The mental picture made her smile as she loaded the dishwasher front to back. While she worked, she looked at Elvis's empty spot. Maybe she'd sneak back and visit him before bedtime.

—

Next morning, Emmet straightened his cereal bowl before pouring Captain Crunch in it. The bowl was half-filled when a yellow scarf fell into the bowl and burst into flames. He leaped away from the table. "What the…?" He turned to Sally. "Are you some kind of witch?"

Sally doused the fire with a glass of water, shaking her head mightily. "No. No. How could I possibly make that happen?" Her lips trembled.

"I should get rid of you just like you got rid of that cutout." He stomped out the door.

Sally watched his car leave the driveway and then hurried back to retrieve Elvis from the closet. The yellow scarf no longer hung around his neck.

She placed him right by the window where the morning sun showed off his stunning face, his upper lip sneering in that way that made her stomach flip-flop.

A few blackened bits of the yellow scarf lay sodden in the bowl. She fished them out and put them on a paper towel to dry.

—

Sally took extra pains with the beef stew, being sure the gravy was neither too thin nor too thick. The potatoes were overdone, just the way Emmet liked them. She added extra butter to melt and heighten the flavors. The stew smelled and tasted delicious. She wanted to sprinkle parsley on top, but Emmet would curse her.

Emmet sat at the table feeding his fat face, gravy smearing his chin. "This is greasier than usual, isn't it?"

Sally stammered. "I added a little butter to bring out the flavors."

"Well, don't." He shoved his empty plate away and left the room.

———

She really needed Elvis tonight. Emmet was wearing her down, little by little, like water reshaping stone. She put her Elvis channel on low while she loaded the dishwasher.

———

Next morning, weary from a sleepless night, Sally placed Emmet's cereal bowl exactly centered in front of his chair. She placed the box of Captain Crunch within easy reach of his right hand, a pitcher of milk next to it. She got his favorite mug from the cupboard and poured it full of freshly brewed coffee.

Emmet came into the kitchen without giving her a glance. He poured his Captain Crunch without incident and adjusted the milk to his liking. When he reached for his favorite mug of coffee, ready to sip, a frown wrinkled his forehead. "There's something crusty stuck to the rim. You should check for that before serving it."

While Sally watched wide-eyed, a red scarf appeared behind Emmet's fat neck. It wound around it, barely long enough, and tightened.

Emmet choked.

The scarf tightened more.

Sally stared in disbelief and sucked in her breath.

Emmet clutched, scrambled, and scratched his neck, trying to pull away the scarf.   The scarf gave one more jerk. Emmet's tongue protruded from his mouth, and his head lolled to the side. The floor shuddered when he fell with a thud.

Sally gasped and clamped her hand over her mouth, feeling faint. With a deep breath, she stooped and put her hands in Emmet's sweaty armpits. Struggling, panting, straining, one backward step followed by another, she dragged Emmet's body to the closet where Elvis waited.

She opened the door, and her savior stood there. No scarves decorated his neck. She grabbed the cutout from the closet, embraced it, clung to it, and covered it with kisses. With her arms and feet, she shoved Emmet's body in the closet. The door shut with difficulty, but at last, it clicked. Sally turned the key in the lock and leaned against it, sweating with relief and exertion.

She took a step to return Elvis to his kitchen spot but set him down and returned to the closet. From Emmet's fat, discolored neck, she removed the red scarf.

—

Elvis stood fine and proud in the morning sunshine.

"There's only one king in this kitchen now."

Sally turned her iPhone up loud as the strains of "Love Me Tender" filled the kitchen, and she loaded the breakfast dishes in the dishwasher, front to back.

The Hat

Russell Reece

No pipes   no faucets nearby
      but a constant   drip   drip   drip
           water oozes onto the table
    I have to make the hat   no escaping that
the newspaper is soaked   soggy sheets fall apart in my hand
      I use   a *Slipknot*   carefully form
        a fedora

    a gangster fedora
       a hat with swagger
         a hat with a fuck you attitude
that   slowly   slowly   slowly
collapses   on the table
       It needs   encouragement
      a band maybe
Motley Crue   *Megadeth*   *Guns and Roses*
  No!   none of those will do   a hat band
    a band for the hat   so the woman

Disturbed   and looking for a fight
                 gets duck tape   from the refrigerator
brings it to me on a plate   bares her yellowed teeth   snarls
     I think   *Bullet for My Valentine*
                                   I unroll the tape   not tape
       a shiny metallic sheet
                              metallic   *Metallica*
No!   that's not it   I need to   cut it   cut it
                 into bands   iron bands   *Iron Maiden*
     No!   not *Iron Maid*en either
                    not for the hat   no escaping that
       but the woman   appears again   angry   agitated
knife in clenched fist
                         staring
                                   at the lump
                                        on the worktable
water   oozing
                                   drip   drip   drip
the woman
                   eyes gleaming
                                   growling
knife shining in her clenched fist
                   stabbing   piercing
                                        the hat   not hat
       stabbing   twisting
          like a slayer   *Slayer!*
              That's the one!

160

Snail! Snail! Show Me Your Horns

J.C. Raye

Bells lashed to an ankle. Cans scraping along ribbed tin. Arms bending slowly, smoothly, pointing skyward. Hips rolling as in the way of water, the way of clouds. Stepping. Turning. Keeping time with other children. Wearing the blue rubber shoes sent from the West.

Clever sits perched on a rock, barely concealed by a tangle of bread grass, gun propped between bony knees. He stares down the hillside, thick with green, at the only standing structure for miles. Convent. *A place,* his commander had said, *that harbors enemy spies. A place of girls.*

He could recall it still, a dance in front of a dusty cloth, the large open courtyard with color handprints on hanging paper. But the picture in his mind seems hazy, as if viewed through dust billows churned up by heavy trucks upon the road. The walls of the compound below are strong, made of brick, not mud and stick, with a locked iron gate to safeguard the precious contents housed within. This is perhaps what makes Clever think of his school days and former life. It seems such a long time ago. He wonders if these are not his own memories at all, but those of some other boy, one he had killed, now come to haunt him. He thinks that, perhaps, they are leftover dreams, bent from tales told by night fire to keep the youngest from crying. Or maybe it's the hunger conjuring these swirling shadows. Hunger can make almost anything happen, as he had well seen.

A violent cuff cups his ear and knocks him sideways, tearing Clever from his pleasant daydream. Germaine stands over Clever and slaps him a second time, harder, and across the cheek. The captain's aim is much better now, and Clever feels a wetness above the bone there.

Clever sees now that Dovis is also there, holding his stomach with both hands. The younger boy's eyes are wet. Germaine shouts at both boys. He demands to know why they should not both be killed for disobeying direct orders, performing his own vibrant dance of sorts, a furious tirade, machete held high in the air against purple clouds swallowing sunset.

Germaine decides he will lead them down to the convent gate himself come morning. He will show them how to act. Show them how to make this whore-nun obey. If lucky, they will be inside the convent before Commander arrives with the others. Germaine orders the boys to build a new fire and stretch a tarp in the trees. He sits and smokes and strategizes for them. While scraping out tinder, Dovis asks if there is any food. Dovis is only eleven and not yet wise enough to know better, as he has been a soldier for merely four months. Germaine fiercely kicks Dovis to the dirt and insists that the boy should not allow his belly to render him useless. Germaine is seventeen, only a few years older than Clever, but has had much more experience and can be very frightening at times. Germaine is a captain, Clever and Dovis are simple foot soldiers, and this is the way of it. Beatings are part of a daily routine, like breathing or taking a shit in the bush. Commander says every beating serves a purpose.

Germaine wears his beret low, tipped to one side, and his hair is dyed blue. He buys the color from the *dawa* woman who visits camp regularly to put spells on their group, chants that will transform enemy bullets into harmless drops of rain. Clever thinks Germaine is quite handsome, except for his constantly shifting eyes. They move as if Germaine is hearing strange broadcasts from the surrounding plants and trees. Clever never seems bothered by heat or stinging insects and always looks neat. Even the blood splashed upon his uniform has dried in patches that make the stains appear intentional, almost stylish. Germaine says he enlisted and was not kidnapped into the militia, but Clever does not believe him. He once saw Germaine twist a blade deeply to dig out the eye of a woman who tried to run from him, and another time, he pumped a whole magazine of bullets into a man for shouting a warning. Commander shot Germaine in the meaty part of his arm for that one and would not allow anyone from camp to remove the bullet. It rests there still, just below the skin. A reminder to all his brothers-in-arms of the high price for wasting ammunition.

———

Clever lived with his family in Birundule before he was taken by Mai-Mai. Before the night, the militia rushed out from the trees to set his village alight, and the shrill screams of women and burning animals could not be told apart. Prior to that evening, he had never been outside of his village. Had never cut through calm water in a pirogue or bumped along muddy trenches on the back of a motorbike or burned his tongue on *pili pili* sauce. Though now, as a soldier, he has done all three.

The early days were harder, of course, when Clever would bury his face in his cap as if resting, all the while crying. March. Fight. Camp. Cook. Same every day. Sleeping in short spurts or not at all. Walk ten steps to move forward five. Hearing fat raindrops that would cool the skin blocked overhead by the humid blanket of green. Biting blackflies. Biting snakes. Some in the militia would get diseases, and there were many sicknesses. One was blinded from a river worm. And when plastic bags did not work properly while crossing water, wet clothes taking the entire day to dry made Clever feel as if he was carrying the weight of a whole other boy on his back. Journeys which almost broke him. But the older ones would always press him on, beat him if necessary. Train him to be strong. They tell him if he is not made straight while he is green, he can never be made straight when he is dry.

Some of his brother soldiers have lived this way, as a fighter in the bush, for more than ten years. And the oldest of these were to be feared, simply because they now feared nothing at all. JeeBe, who once let a giant spider sleep on his chest all night. Manassé, who keeps track of enemy kills by slicing marks into his arms. Clever imagines one day he will be braver, too. Sometimes the younger ones are given beer to drink, to avoid their worry when going to the front. One can only go to the front feeling very strong in the mind. Commander says that in fighting, there can be no pity. He tells them all that they have emerged from the era of dictatorships and politicians, grown children who still are only big liars. *People,* he attests, *are now waking up to that fact, and we must take the reins.*

Elders are not wise any longer, for if they were, we would not be in this state. It may take another few years, maybe five at the most, but things are going to change in this country. Clever does not always understand what these words mean, but the Mai-Mai are his only family now, and the commander says he is their honest father, and they must all trust him.

Of course, there are easier days. Good days to be a soldier. When camp is low on supplies, a group is sent to block the road, set up a checkpoint, while others are stationed hillside to watch for the *blue helmets*. On these days, trucks and cars are taxed; men on motorcycles are ordered to pay a license fee. Few civilians resist, and most are generous. They know the militia watches over them and keeps them safe, so people will give what they have. Francs. Kerosene. Bags filled with brown palm oil. Beans. Occasionally, some villager will argue, make an excuse, saying that his children starve, or the items he transports are not his own, but these are surely collaborators. Clever does not yet have the strength to chop off a limb with one swipe, but he has become quite good at cutting off ears. The bodies of the dead are then placed across the road so that they are seen and must be moved. *It sends a message*, Commander says.

———

The night before the slap on the hill, Clever is sitting around a fire at their camp. He is listening to the older boys speak while they drink the sodas found in a hut, before they burn it, before Manassé chops the owner, a village elder who was most certainly a conspirator. Some hear the man mention a convent full of girls nearby run by a woman named Sister Joy. *A witch who only dresses as a nun*, Manassé says. He says *looking into her eyes can cause you to fall dead or develop sores over your body.* And that *she does not need to touch you to make this happen.*

Many in the circle seem to have heard of the nun. They nod and share stories of her curses and the poison of her touch. The younger boys become afraid. JeeBe is tall and lanky, and his body always sways on his feet as if moved by wind, even when there is none. Though he is twenty-two, his face is still that of a boy. He speaks very little, and when he does, it is only to repeat what the commander has said, so he is not very good to listen to. JeeBe insists it is better to die a soldier, so your parents can be proud. Your friends, too, will also be proud. But to die as a civilian means to die at the hands of a machete, and that is a stupid and pointless death. Another soldier laughs and says one should make sure to bring a sharp knife to the fight as the nun is said to have a long beard. Germaine spits orange into the fire and says it will be something soft to rest his forehead on when he fucks her. Everyone laughs, even Commander.

Commander decides that in the morning, two soldiers will be dispatched to the convent and prepare it for the militia's arrival in two days' time. The soldiers are to build a fire close by and throw a cartridge into the flame. The trick will convince those within the convent that many soldiers and guns surround them. They will give what is wanted more peacefully. Clever and Dovis are chosen. Their smooth, innocent faces will lure Sister Joy into opening the locked gate. The commander laughs and pats Germaine on the back, adding, *A cat can go to a monastery, but she remains a cat.* The two laugh as if they share a secret. Clever believes that Germaine will one day be a commander, too.

———

Clever and Dovis had not disobeyed orders. They had exploded the cartridge and gone to the convent gate and seen the many girls inside crowding the courtyard. Playing and jumping rope. Sitting. Sewing. They do not see any

boys or men or even older people inside, and Clever feels full of relief and courage since there is no one to
resist. A group of girls stands in a circle and tosses a ball between them. Their song was one Clever had not heard in many years.

> *Escargot! Escargot!*
> *Montre moi tes cornes*
> *Ou sinon, je te mets*
> *Dans la casserole!*

The girls see the two soldiers through the bars and begin to call out. They look afraid. Clever shouts, putting great strength to his voice, the same way he's heard his fellow fighters issue commands to villagers:

We are Mai-Mai! You will let us in! You will bring the nun!

Dovis does not know what to say. He raises his gun into the air mimicking Clever's movement. The boys point their weapons at anyone who moves. They bang the guns against the iron and try to make a fearful impression, though they have not yet learned how to shoot. Commander has taught that much can be done by simply creating fear in the mind, a feat that can be accomplished without the use of bullets.

And then *she* appears. In an open doorway. Sister Joy. Not draped in white habit with her hair covered as described by the others, and not adorned in bold, bright colors of kitenge. Instead, she wears pants and a man's button shirt, with sleeves rolled up. Black. The fabric hugs her thick body like an even layer of bark around a Tola tree. A pink measuring ribbon is draped around her neck. No cross. No praying beads. Her smoke-silver hair is worn in a tight halo, and Clever sees plainly that she has no beard.

The nun walks straight up to the gate. She does not stop to offer soothing words to the girls or shoo them inside for safety. Her footfalls are not sauntering. She *marches*. Clever does not think she carries herself as a nun should, as a woman should. With some dread of them. With respect. Hers is a fearless behavior, and it sends a strange chill up Clever's spine despite the boil of day's sun. He knows there will be a problem.

The yard is strangely silent as Sister Joy closes the distance, except for a chime of small bells swinging somewhere nearby but out of sight. Clever orders Sister Joy to unlock the gate. He explains that a truck will arrive to take away supplies needed for the militia, which are to be ready in piles just inside. He tells her that the Mai-Mai are defending the territory from dangerous forces. Clever does not tell Sister Joy that the vehicle will also take some of her girls or that the commander will order her body hacked to pieces, her skull ground to dust, and her bones and teeth scattered so she cannot return from the dead.

Sister Joy's eyes are slanted and wideset and give the impression she can see in many directions at once. A hack scar stretches from just under her right eye to the bottom of her chin. It looks to be a very old scar, and it gives Clever a powerful feeling she will not be swayed by his words or by the showing of weapons. Sister Joy stares straight into Clever's eyes and tells both boys to go home, to find what is left of their families, and go to school. *Leave these madmen to their schemes.* She tells them she can see their eyes are already full of blood, and their brains are cloudy with hate. *Passing through this gate will forever change who you are.* And though the nun's words may have been meant as advice, her voice, full of rasp, has a slithery sound to it, as if she wants them to enter her convent. To Clever, it sounds like a dare.

Clever and Dovis have no other strategy. They have guns with no bullets and machetes, which are useless against iron bars.

The young soldiers panic and retreat to the nearby hillside.

———

Once, Clever's militia camp was visited by a tall white man who pleaded for Commander to *demobilize* a few of the children. This word meant that they could rejoin civilian life and would no longer have guns and no longer fight. Clever watched the visitor speak to his translator, lips barely opening wide enough to slip a cassava leaf through. The emerging sound was a continuous, rolling buzz, the drone of a bothersome insect. The exchange reminded Clever that he would like to attend school again. Perhaps one day have a good job, better than a fighter. Work in a hospital or maybe a brewery.

Though he was in camp, Commander made the man and his translator wait two hours before he would meet with them. To show them who was in charge out here. They were eventually brought into the round hut, with guns pointed at their heads in case they should try to force the issue. The heat within the hut was oppressive, and heads dripped. Commander sat on a spring-cushioned chair, as scarlet as the seeds of a lucky bean plant, sipping a beer and wearing a black cowboy hat. The white man said that the children looked tired, that Commander should give them a better life. He talked a long time and grew increasingly frustrated while his white face turned rose-colored. In the end, he paid many francs for Commander to release only. Clever and Medy. Medy was the smallest and was missing a piece of his upper lip.

A short ceremony was held outside of a sleeping tent where the two boys were demobilized. The entire militia stood and saluted them, and they turned in their guns. The stranger and his interpreter then put Clever and Medy in a car and drove them to a center with a tattered, sky-blue flag hanging out front and many other demobilized boys inside, even some girls. It had no locked gate. The boys were given food and cots with coils, and they were examined by a stern doctor who said their bones were, bit by bit, eating out their bodies. Clever did not understand what this meant or why the man punched a table and walked out of the room.

Later that day, when the buzzy-voiced man and translator departed the center, some of Clever's brother soldiers arrived and said Commander had decided he could not spare the boys after all. They were needed for an important and upcoming militia offensive. Clever and Medy were returned to camp and given their guns by nightfall. Commander told Clever not to be sorrowful, for the Mai-Mai now held vast territory in North Kivu, and soon every soldier would each receive a car carried in by ferry for their sacrifices. Commander explained that on that day, a celebration of victory would occur. They would eat meat shawarma sandwiches and let the oily juices drip down their chins.

———

Clever watches Germaine run along the roof of the convent, gun balanced in one hand, body bent low. A tin roof covers the sleeping building, and it supports Germaine's weight. His skinny frame bobs up and down against the new sun, and he looks to Clever as if he's a bird, bounding across the forest floor to collect furnishings for a mud nest. Germaine hunkers down for a moment, then rises quickly to hurl a grenade. He drops onto his stomach and covers his head and ears with his arms. The explosion brings up chunks of earth from a point below where Clever cannot see. The explosion also brings up screams. It sends a message.

Now the iron gate is open when the fighters approach. A small pile of food rests on the ground, just inside the entrance of the convent, where it can easily be spotted. Clean white sacks of wheat flour. Powdered milk. Large silver cans of vegetable oil. This time, the nun's head is bowed down in respect as Clever and Dovis brush past her and continue into the yard. The girls await them there. They do not cry or cower, hold each other's hands or heads. They simply stand. Clever thinks it is a strangely silent victory.

Sister Joy has not touched the bodies. They remain where they first fell even though she has had ample time to tend to the dead. The limbs of one are splayed out as if at rest, but above the shoulders, there is nothing. From there, a narrow creeklet of blood has fingered its way along clumps of gray earth to meet the head, which is split in two and several feet away. Another girl has been transformed into a pulped mash, mingled with yellow cotton dress fabric, except for one arm, which still bears a small bracelet of mixed-color wood beads. Clever feels nothing about this, but he can see horror in Dovis's eyes. It is a hard lesson to learn, but it is the way of things. Civilians must appease the militia who protect them.

Germaine places a foot on the topmost sack of the provisions. He tells Sister Joy to arrange the girls in a row, short to tall. He says the militia needs help to cook and clean. Even before they are lined up properly, Clever can see that Germaine has already picked out several of the prettiest. Clever can even tell which one Germaine likes best, which girl will be the first to scream this night. He also chooses one who is not pretty but with large arms and shoulders for toting heavy items. Clever and Dovis point their guns at the selected girls and motion for them to leave the line.

But now, the gun seems heavy and burdensome in Clever's arms as never before, as if he no longer knows how to hold it properly. He feels a tearing slash across his upper chest, sees the fabric of his uniform there *move*. A busyness there which is not right. More pain follows, sharper, twisting, and down below, between his legs. He drops the gun and screams as a hailstorm of fierce needles poke fiery rows into his scalp. He reaches up, expecting to swat at what must be a legion of angry wasps. But Clever does not find bugs. Rather, he finds softness, he finds length, his fingers caught in a silky web. He does not understand. The pain in his groin grows more intense. It is excruciating. It stops him from taking in breath.

Instinctively, Clever turns to Dovis just in time to watch the boy's tongue fall out. The pink, blubbery bundle smacks the dust. He sees the youngster's eyes widen in terror as a small hand rushes to cover an open, bleeding mouth. Dovis drops. Perhaps in agony. Perhaps in the thought of recovering his organ. Sobbing, mewling, he crawls about in wild circles. Before he can reach down to his companion, Clever is spun around by strong hands. It is Germaine. Or what had been Germaine. His uniform shirt, always so neat, is tattered, torn open from within by newly formed breasts that lightly bounce in the sunlight. A new, wider bone structure around his hips snap his belt off. He is howling into Clever's face, but blood does not line Germaine's lips because *his* tongue has been swallowed.

The entire metamorphosis, which seemed an eternity, the unspeakable level of torture from which one should not even survive, has, in truth, lasted only minutes. The three attractive girls, new to the convent, have no marks upon them to indicate that anything has occurred at all. Except that they can no longer speak. Sister Joy, not witch, not whore, not woman, is suddenly upon them, bearing bright dresses for their newly curved figures and wraps for their fresh, luscious hair. She works quickly.

Sister Joy is tucking in the corners of Clever's headscarf when the militia arrives to collect both food and girls. The large military vehicle pulls through the gate. Commander steps out first and scans the yard. Clever follows his eyes and sucks in a hard breath. He can already see the girl whom Commander has chosen for himself.

And yes, Germaine is by far the prettiest.

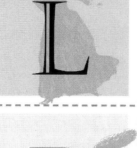

The
FANCIFUL
and
CONFOUNDING
HALLOWEEN
PARTY
PUZZLE
PAGE

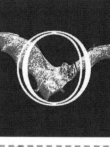

DIRECTIONS

1. Using scissors, carefully cut out each square.
2. Recycle the paper scraps.
3. Pause for cool refreshment.
4. Unscramble the letters.
5. Celebrate your success.

Elevator of Blood

Robert Fleming

FADE IN!
Such a set setup:
      make 1,000 gallons of blood,
            red dye, red dye, red dye!
contain blood, in buckets;
Kubrick commands:
      Make enough blood 4 10 takes!
      Don't let the blood drip into the gap!
ACTION!
Drain the blood on the elevator floor.
CUT!
Supermop the floor, for the next take,
Cut! MORE blood! Action!
Cut! LESS blood! Action!
Stanley smiles, Tomkins, the Blood's, right;
FINAL CLOT!

UCLA film school did not teach me,
      how to remove a blood wave,
            from delivered egg carpet!
Next setup:
      the twins tricycling,
            on the yellow carpet,
                and linoleum floor:

Extract the blood drops from the carpet!
SHINE the linoleum!
Stanley says, Jack, start Shining!
Tomkins says, Tricycle Set's Set
Kubrick screams:
      Twins on Tricycles, Take #1,
          Alcott shoot,
             ACTION!

FADE OUT!

A Good Daughter

Kim DeCicco

Each step I take echoes down the hall of this public mausoleum. I pass hundreds of carved, gold-leafed names, but only one matters—my mother s. Her body is encased behind a marble plaque and rests in section 32; second crypt from the left, third row from the bottom, forty-nine steps from the entrance.

Almost every September 17th, for the past eight years, I've come here to pay homage to my mother. I begin each visit by pressing my lips to her three-by-five portrait, which is affixed below a vase mounted next to her name. I then place a single peony in that vase. My mother loved peonies. I never understood them. While their beauty is evident, their heavy flowers make no sense. As soon as they bloom, their weighty petals bow them over. They have but a moment of glory, and perhaps that is their message: as soon as you blossom, stress pulls you down. My mother was only 48 when she died, her bloom only beginning to fade.

Today I sit on the floor across from her crypt, my back against "Lily Ambrose, Always Remembered," writing these words in a journal at the suggestion of my therapist. Her theory is that if I commit my feelings and these episodes to paper, I will see they are nothing more than the various stages of grief and not the haunted encounters I claim to have had.

I will start at the beginning.

The first year I visited my mother's crypt, my sobs weighted each footfall as I walked along a path to the heavy brass doors of the mausoleum. I still missed her so terribly that I couldn't make it through the portal. The office secretary, Esther, found me weeping uncontrollably on the marble steps of the entrance. She collected me in her arms and rocked me as a mother would her child. To this day, I bring her a bottle of merlot as part of my pilgrimage. I hope she understands how her simple kindness shored me up enough to complete my task.

I was able to make it through the doors of the mausoleum without breaking down on my second year's visit. That year I told my mother how I had applied to a performing arts college. As soon as those words were out of my mouth, I experienced an odd tingle up my back, and I saw something in my periphery. A shudder ran through my body. Someone was behind me. I spun around but found myself alone.

Nerves, I thought. My mother had been against my desire to pursue dance as a career, as well as to go into the city for schooling. "You don't want to travel for college," she said once. "I'll never see you. Anyway, dancing is a hobby, not something that requires a degree."

I shook my head to clear my mind, but my unease had progressed to nausea. I walked to the office located just inside the entrance and asked Esther if she'd seen anyone else in the building. "I felt as if I was being watched," I told her.

"Maybe it was the witch," said a voice from behind me.

"What?" I turned and encountered a man with long gray hair and a scruffy beard wearing dirt-covered jeans.

He offered his hand. "Lenny Connor, groundskeeper, and I said maybe it was the witch."

A little confused, I took his proffered hand, felt his rough calluses against my skin, but looked to Esther for explanation. She reached under the counter, retrieved a two-page pamphlet, and handed it to me.

"Legend says," she began, "that beneath this mausoleum, deep in the ground, lie the bones of a witch. A woman who, in 1705, was beaten unrecognizable because people claimed she had cursed them. The story tells us that her broken body was dragged to this spot and left to die, to rot, and to sink into unconsecrated earth. At the time, this land was dank forest on the outskirts of the village. The townspeople expected she would be forgotten. Instead," Esther said, "she walks through time and through these halls."

"You don't really believe that."

She shrugged her shoulders, but it was the groundskeeper who replied.

"Why not? Other visitors and some staff said they've experienced the same feeling. Plus"—he smiled—"gruesome tales bring in extra funding around Halloween in the form of ghost tours."

"I see," I said, although I didn't. I thanked them and returned to my car to read the story.

The pamphlet contains a shortened version of a tale originally written in 1842 by Hildegard Van Faulk, who alleged that her great-great-grandmother heard the story in her youth from an irrefutable eyewitness—the witch's daughter, who had been unknown to all until many years later.

I include the pamphlet here for reference:

Hester, whom today some would call "witch," was referred to in her time as a cunning woman. She lived near the forest outside of the village, and her advice was often sought for the various ailments that afflicted humans and livestock. Hester had a misshapen child, a daughter named Sarah, who she kept leashed to their house with a rope tied around Sarah's waist and then attached to an exposed ceiling beam. When anyone came by, the daughter was unbound, herded into the root cellar, and told to be quiet. She was a good daughter. She always did what her mother wished.

One fall evening, people were heard coming toward the house. Hester pushed Sarah into the cellar. Sarah said she'd heard several men shouting and the door bang open. Then she heard a thwack, and something heavy hit the floor. She heard groans and muffled thumps. She knew they were beating her mother, and although it broke her heart, she remained silent and hidden. Her mother had insisted she do so, and she was a good daughter.

Once the villagers left, that good daughter crept from the cellar and looked for her mother. Not finding her in their abode, Sarah followed a trail of blood out the door and into the woods. She found her mother, bloodied and without breath, in a heap on the ground. Sarah opened her mouth in a silent scream. She pulled at her hair. She wept without a sound.

Sarah, bent and crippled, scraped at the ground with a piece of shale. She dug a shallow grave and rolled the mother to whom she had been so closely bound in life into the ditch, adjusting her so she rested on her back. That good daughter pulled an oval, wood-framed mirror from the folds of her worn dress to which she had fastened leather straps so she could attach it to a gourd or a pillow to keep her company in the root cellar or on long winter nights. She placed the mirror over her mother's shattered face, tying the straps tightly behind her mother's head. Sarah's own dirt-stained face reflected back, and she smiled. This was good. She would forever shine in Mother's eyes.

I shivered when I read those last words and thought, *How creepy*. I tossed the pamphlet into the backseat and started my car. As I drove home, I wondered if I was also still trying to "shine" in my mother's eyes. My nausea increased. I was probably being paranoid. A dull ache started to blossom in my head. A migraine was coming on.

When I went to visit my mother on the third anniversary of her death, I told her I realized she'd been right. Going to college for dance was fanciful. I had changed my mind, stayed home, and studied accounting—as she'd once suggested. Boring, yes, but steady and lucrative work. But the more important news was that I had met someone at school and was to be married. Our shy beginnings had blossomed into a torrid affair of blinding lust and clutching love. We could not see the world outside of ourselves. While I sat relating my newly found happiness to my mother, a silhouette shimmered in the corner of my eye. Nothing was there when I snapped my head around, but the air seemed to sizzle with hostility and press down on me as if the very space was angry.

I knew my mother would have been upset by my decision to marry if she were alive.

"A man will take the best years of your life in the hope of breeding sons, then he'll leave you if you don't." That's what she'd often told me. That's what she said had happened to her and why I never knew my father.

Mom? Are you here?" I asked the empty hall. Of course, there was no response.

"I'm being ridiculous," I said into the heavy air. Then I heard a distinct clink, followed by a slow and steady plop . . . plop . . . plop. The vase holding the peony had cracked and was dripping water.

Every hair on my body rose.

I ran to the office.

"The vase broke!" I told Esther as I gripped the counter's edge. "The air sizzled and became thick, then the vase broke." My eyes wide and wild, I blurted, "I think it was my mother's ghost."

She gave me a sad look. "You sorely miss her."

181

"Of course I do."

"Would you wish her back?"

"Yes, I feel lost without her."

"I understand. Daughters will miss their mothers." She gave me a placating smile. "But don't worry about ghosts. What you felt is the air conditioning system. It needs tending. And the vases are faulty, thin. They crack easily, usually due to vibrations from the excavator as it passes the building."

I felt like a fool and tried to recover some credibility. "With all of the groundskeeper's talk about witches last time, thinking my mother decided to haunt the place seemed reasonable." I flashed her a grin and hoped my cheeks didn't look as flushed as they felt.

"No, your mother isn't haunting the mausoleum," Lenny said as he sidled up next to me and patted the hand I still had on the counter. "But it could be the witch."

"Esther said it was the excavator."

"She said it's *usually* the excavator."

I jerked my hand away. "Are you deliberately trying to upset me?"

He sighed, tugged at his beard. "No, but I spend most of my days alone and surrounded by the dead. I've developed a dark sense of humor."

"Well, please don't use it with me." I tugged my jacket straight with a huff and left the office. I sent a departing glance toward my mother's crypt and saw that the peony had curled and withered to brown. A few petals had fluttered to the floor. A chill ran up my spine. That shouldn't have happened so quickly. It should've taken at least a day, even without water in the vase. I spun away and rushed through the exit. I'd had enough spooky for one day.

When I went to visit my mother in the fifth year, I told her how the relationship with my husband was breaking apart. He said I was no longer fun because I put housework before intimacy, savings before vacations, and leftovers before a fresh meal. I didn't understand his criticism. My mother taught me to clean up each night before bed, to stay debt-free, to never waste food. He didn't understand when I told him I didn't feel sexy if I knew the kitchen wasn't set straight for the night, that I couldn't relax on a vacation knowing the cost would incur debt, that I was morally opposed to throwing away food just because we had it a night or two before. He felt he couldn't live with such strict rules. I felt this was how responsible people should be. He didn't agree and pulled further and further away from me.

That fifth year I told my mother of my fear that he would leave, of my fear of being alone—of my fear that maybe, just maybe, I had married him to fill the void left by her death. Again, I cried out my grief to a marble floor. And again, a knowing hand stroked my back with sympathy. I had done the best I could with my sodden tissue and lifted my head to thank Esther for her kindness.

But instead of seeing Esther, I was greeted by a translucent figure with a black-spotted mirror for a face. My open-mouthed horror reflected back at me as the walls undulated with the reverberation of my screams.

Soon it *was* Esther who crouched over me, but she stumbled back as my rantings about a ghostly vision with a mirrored face became more hysterical. Unable to console me, she threatened to call an ambulance. "They will sedate you," she said.

I clamped my hands over my mouth. Tears of fright spilled from my eyes as I sought control. I didn't relish the idea of being drugged, or worse, being ferried to a hospital. I put my head between my knees and lengthened my breaths. My rapidly beating heart began to slow.

A crash from the office jolted me upright and sent my heart slamming against my ribs once more. Esther hurried to investigate. I rose slowly and followed, using the wall of crypts as support for each step.

When I peered into the office, I saw Lenny and Esther tossing broken glass into a wastebasket. An oval frame was visible over its rim.

"It was you!" I pointed at Lenny. "What kind of twisted person are you?"

"It wasn't him," Esther said as she took hold of my shoulders with her frail hands. "He accidentally knocked a painting from the wall. Here." She pulled an old, pastoral scene from the trash bin and held it out to me. "See?"

I looked at the picture, then at the pieces of clear glass, not mirror, in the garbage. This couldn't have been what I saw. "I'm sorry," I said to Lenny.

He smirked, then made circular motions next to his head while mouthing the word, "Cuckoo," at me.

I ran from the mausoleum. I had to get away from that crazy groundskeeper, as well as the lingering grief that surrounded the place.

Once home and ensconced on my couch with tea and a blanket, I told my husband what happened. Idiotic groundskeeper aside, my husband was convinced that what I saw had to be the result of stress—a figment conjured by an over-wrought imagination. He felt I d been living my life wrapped completely in grief and demanded I seek help. With a prompt call to his coworker, whose wife was a therapist, he had me an appointment for two days later.

My husband left me soon after. My "hallucination," the word he and my therapist used to describe what happened at the mausoleum, was the last straw. I spent the year focused on healing from my divorce and the loss of my mother. During this time, I recognized that I had been enveloped with angst from the moment of my mother's death. Without her to mold me into the form she envisioned, I had lived my life filled with doubt about who I was, what I wanted, and how to navigate my future. She had spun a web around me during her life, a cocoon in which to hold me—not out of love, but from a need to control. I was bound to her so strongly while she lived that I remained indentured after her death.

It was time to cut those bonds. It was time to let my mother go.

Now, on this sixth anniversary of my mother's death, I come to bid her farewell. I will tell her I go forward as myself, for myself. No longer will I feel forced to live the life she wanted.

———

I write this to make a record of what happened to Diana Torby.

Diana came to Ocean View Cemetery to visit her mother's remains annually for the past six years. Today, Diana's last day here, I watched from the office doorway as she lay this journal on the floor. I watched as she placed a flower in the vase next to her mother's name. I watched as she kissed her mother's image. I watched as she stood in front of the plaque enclosing her mother's bones and whispered, "Your hold on me is over. I'm not coming back."

When she made to leave, the air began to crackle. A dense fog gathered and swirled between where she stood and from where I observed. It became a thick, black funnel and spewed a rage that hummed along my skin. The concentrated storm exploded with a deafening blast that slammed Diana into a wall of crypts and sent pieces of marble raining down. Protected in the office doorway, I saw that the marble plaque in front of Diana's mother's vault had blown apart, and two skeleton hands clutched the sides of the opening. The smell of earth and decay filled my nose as the top of a filthy skull emerged from the hole. Bony fingers dug into the creviced names engraved in the plaque above, leverage for a black-clad torso to pull itself out. The ghastly figure griped other names to twist itself around until it hung over the crypts below. It slid from the tomb and down the wall.

The wraith crawled toward Diana. Dirty bone feet peeked from beneath the hem of its ragged black dress, and a spotted oval mirror covered its face. I blinked, and the figure was three feet closer to Diana, moving like the flickering pictures of a silent movie. I was mesmerized by the terror on Diana's face. Her countenance was so deformed by horror that I could hardly believe it was still her.

Fleshless fingers tugged at straps binding the mirror to the figure's head. Once free, the specter lowered the mirror, inch by inch, to reveal a broken chamber where its face had been. The jaw—attached on one side only because an ancient root had become a coiled hinge—swung at random as it spoke.

"A good daughter always does what Mother wants."

The figure curled a bony hand around Diana's head and leaned into her as if for a kiss. It began to inhale, drawing life from Diana and into itself. Any struggles were thwarted by its other arm wrapped around Diana's waist, the mirror pressed hard into Diana's back.

Diana's body became compressed, dehydrated, but her eyes remained panicked. I believe she could still see. She sat frozen and helpless as the figure, now a young, living woman bearing Diana s face, lifted the mirror, placed it in front of Diana's eyes, and strapped it tightly around her head.

"You should have been more careful, Daughter," the woman said. "The dead are restless. They will take you if given the chance."

Lenny closed the journal and watched Esther rotate the vase-mount on Lily Ambrose's crypt a quarter turn. He heard a soft click and the marble plaque popped out enough for Esther to pull it forward, revealing a drawer inside.

He walked over and placed Diana's journal, the journal in which he had been writing, on top of dozens of other diaries, letters, and various memorabilia that had been collected over the centuries.

"A good daughter's sacrifice should always be remembered," Esther said as she pushed the drawer closed.

"I guess," Lenny said as he lifted Diana's lifeless body and began stuffing her into her mother's crypt.

"Is there a problem?"

"Yeah! You said I could have this one." He gave Diana one last shove. The only part of her still visible were the soles of her shoes. "I'm getting too old to keep up with this job."

"I see." Esther steepled her fingers together in front of her lips, a gesture she made when thinking. After a few moments, she said, "We need to finish here, so get the lift with the new plaque. I'll help you install it, and then we'll talk."

In silence, Lenny retrieved the items, and together they sealed the crypt with silicon caulking and a plastic interior cover. They set the marble front-piece in place and secured each corner with bronze, rosette screws. The new plaque had already been engraved with Diana's mother's name and a fresh portrait and vase-mount added. Once the crumbled remains of the old plaque were cleared away, no one would know anything had happened.

Still in silence, Lenny knelt down to gather pieces of broken marble into a bucket.

Esther heard him sniffle. "Are you crying?"

He made no answer.

"Oh, my poor boy," Esther said as she moved behind him and cradled his head against her abdomen.

Lenny began to weep in earnest. "Why, Mother? Why did you take her?"

Esther slid a hand under his chin as she leaned down to whisper in his ear, "Because I never intended to share eternal life with you." She snapped his neck with a hard, quick twist.

She guided Lenny's limp body to the floor, then consulted her watch: 6:00 p.m. She had a long night ahead. Digging a grave was tedious work, plus she had to deal with the mess still in the mausoleum hall. She already missed Lenny's help, but he had become a liability—too old for the physical labor and, certainly, too needy.

Esther double-checked that the entrance was locked then sought out heavy boots from the storeroom behind the office. As she passed the bathroom, she caught her reflection in the mirror. Turning on the overhead light, she moved into the room for a closer look. Diana's eyes stared back. It was always unnerving, seeing someone else's face where hers should be. It took some getting used to.

Pretty, Esther thought as she touched her foreign cheek, but that was a given. She never chose ugly girls. So much easier to attract a mate when one is fetching, and that gave her the chance to breed her own sacrifice. Assuming a stranger's identity could be tricky, so it was best to make a child of her own then take its life when the time was right. But Esther hadn't produced a daughter this time, so Diana had been a godsend. Her lack of family and deep-seated insecurities had made her ripe for the taking.

Back in the hall, Esther looked down at Lenny and sighed. Her son. What a shame she had to kill him. He had been so useful around the cemetery. It was also a shame to have wasted his death, but using a male to regenerate might cost her the ability to give birth, and that was not an option.

Not for a moment would Esther have given Lenny the chance at immortality. She didn't want the competition, but in reality, she didn't know how. She hadn't known such a thing was possible until it happened to her, and she still remained unclear about how it occurred.

Centuries ago, when Esther was known as Hester, it seemed her daughter Sarah enabled her to come back. Each tear Sarah wept over Hester's grave soaked into the earth and awoke in Hester a need to return, a compulsion to resume the discipline of her child. Who was to educate Sarah, if not Hester? What wickedness might now taint Sarah with her mother gone for so long?

What a shock they both received one fateful night when Hester's decayed skeleton sprung from the ground as Sarah cried over the grave.

Sarah's joy was so great that the fool child embraced her mother and knocked the mirror with its rotted straps from Hester's face. Sarah tried to kiss her mother, and that was her last mistake. The cavern where Hester's lips should have been latched on to Sarah's grieving soul and sucked it dry.

Hester caught her reflection in the fallen mirror as she laid her daughter atop the grave. Sarah's face shone from the glass. *Amazing,* Hester thought. Not only was she alive, but she had somehow become her daughter, deformed leg and all.

A few days later, Hester/Sarah journeyed to the village seeking refuge. She explained to the townsfolk that she was Hester's daughter, and while they were shocked and suspicious of her, Sarah's soft nature and crippled leg garnered their pity. She was given a place in their world and soon married and gave birth to a daughter—a daughter who cleaved to her mother as a child should. When Sarah's husband died, she and her young daughter moved away. "The daughter" moved back when "Sarah" died, and the cycle continued.

Esther thought about how limitless her opportunities were as she hoisted Lenny onto a casket trolly and pushed it outside. Consume one child in order to live again, then make another, over and over. She'd been doing it for more than 300 years.

She cranked the trolly lift so she could load Lenny onto a pickup truck.

She'd drive him to a recent burial. The digging would be easier. Esther noticed her forearm was still covered by the decayed black dress, so she shook it until the image disappeared. The mirror-wearing figure was a glamour, a spell, to make her look as she did when she first rose from the earth hundreds of years ago. It wouldn't do for a mother to get caught sucking the soul from her daughter, but the ghost of an ancient witch could do anything.

secOnd Date

Morgan Golladay

"What should we do with the body?" I was careful to ask Daniel in my best clueless Southern drawl. "I've never really been in this situation before, where there is a rather dead body in my house. It's not taking up a lot of room, at least, but it will start to smell in a few days, and God knows, I definitely don't want those neighbors nosing around again! The last time they were here was to invite me over for drinks and hors d'oeuvres. Not my cup of tea, if you'll pardon the expression."

Daniel sat on the opposite end of the couch. The living room curtains were closed against prying eyes, but the night was still young, and there was a whisper of heavy satisfaction and excitement in the air. He couldn't keep his eyes off of me. My skin radiated heat, my cheeks blushed with the roses of youth, and my dewy complexion was breathtaking tonight.

I had met him at his nightclub, the Den, several weeks earlier, and we had hit it off over Cosmopolitans. I had finally asked him over for dinner, hoping

I wouldn't seem too eager, and he asked if he could bring the main course, since he had a long list of connections from his club, and an aperitif to clear our palates. We had a magnificent dinner. Both of us felt invigorated and renewed and ready for whatever adventures the night would bring.

"Daniel, come on! Bring your eyes up here. I'm deadly serious. There's this dead body in my kitchen, and you HAVE to help me get rid of it! Are you absolutely sure no one saw y'all come in tonight?"

"Calm down, Marie, Calm DOWN! We'll be fine," he murmured reassuringly. "I've done this before. There were no lights on next door, and Powell walked in of his own accord. I made sure he would be quiet when I slipped a roofie into his beer at the club. It was fairly easy to get him into my car. And the rest was even easier. He didn't make a sound when we slashed into him; he just lay there with those sad puppy-dog eyes and let us do as we pleased.

"We'll move him out to the garage. Do you have an old tarp or shower curtain to wrap him up in? I've got some tape and large trash bags in the Rover if we need them. Tomorrow night we can take him out in the woods and bury him. Or would you rather take a moonlight cruise with me?" He raised his eyebrows seductively. "The moon is full, and my boat is tied up in this little marina at the bay. It would be fairly easy to run out past the inlet and dump the body in the channel. That might be best. A little romance on the water would be a good cover for dumping the body. Whaddya say? Shovels or sailing?"

I had to think quickly. "Sailing, I guess. I don't want to wait too long. My energy is high, and I don't want any evidence lying around. I've always killed my marks out in the streets. Alleys, dark cover in parks, deserted buildings. Leaving the bodies where the rats and scavengers will have first go at 'em. Create enough mess that no one could guess what really killed them, even if someone cared enough to report them missing."

"Good choice," Daniel responded. "Scootch over here, you gorgeous vixen, you. My energy is so high a roofie couldn't stop me! And I can't wait to let you see just how much I love your hospitality! But I can't stay long. Once we move the body, I want to make a run to the boat and make sure we have enough gas for our midnight run tomorrow. You know how it is. Gotta get home before the morning rush! Damn, I wish these summer nights were longer!"

—

I had parked my car on the street to give Daniel room to back his Range Rover up to the garage door. It was a status car, reflecting Dan's opinion of his own power and standing. We had stripped Powell's body of clothing and identification, rolled it into a heavy plastic tarp, and securely wrapped it with duct tape. It was pretty watertight, and I was proud of our work. It was a lot easier than I'd thought it would be. I'd made a mental note to put this in my report. I also made a mental note regarding the way Daniel's muscles rippled under his polo shirt. This image would stay in the back of my head, giving me lots of reasons to miss sleep over the next few days.

"You know, Marie, you're a lot stronger than you look! I don't guess anyone would even imagine you could handle a 220-pound dead weight like it was a loaf of bread. I'm very impressed! Do you have a special training program or something?" Daniel laughed.

I may be only 5'4", but I'm a lot more than a buxom brunette. A lot more.

"Oh, it's the diet, Dan. You know, the fresher, the better! And eating lower on the food chain. I wonder if this is what they mean by a 'paleo' diet?" I made sure to giggle coyly at my own joke. Dan had already obtained some cinder blocks and a length of poly rope to weigh the body down. I grabbed the picnic basket and my overnight bag and hopped up into the SUV. "Wow! Nice car, Dan! You can really make a statement in this!"

"Gotta keep the profile up! You know, successful nightclub owner, high roller, mover and shaker. On the streets, you're judged as much by what you drive as what you wear."

And Dan's clothes and shoes spoke of power, status, and money.

We arrived at the marina in about 15 minutes. "I chose this place because it's small. They can't pay their staff much, so they only have daytime attendants. It gives me the freedom from prying eyes that I need. That's why you didn't see anyone around when we got here." And there was no one else around when we clambered onto the boat. Powell was quickly loaded, and Dan moved his car to its assigned parking spot.

When he got back, I had changed into a bikini and tossed a light sweater over my shoulders, more for show than anything else, since I seldom got cold. "Just in case," I said.

I could see Dan eyeing me hungrily. We chased the moon across the bay to the inlet, and Dan steered into the channel. "Water's a lot deeper here, and bodies sink so far they'll never be found. Let's say 'farewell and bon appétit' to Powell, and the rest of this night is ours."

———

Less than an hour later, we were back in the inlet. We'd made pretty good time, for we were 250 pounds lighter, and the hull of this 42-foot boat slipped easily through the water. There was a light breeze, and the engine purred with a full-throated hum. I felt like a great weight had been lifted off my shoulders. I could see Dan watching the sky expectantly, planning his next move, and I knew what was coming. He slowed the motor, and we coasted to a still spot in the cove.

After a quick dip to wash off the dirt, I shook my long, dark curls out and finger-combed them into a sort of submission. Daniel's swim trunks were almost dry from when I had eased Powell's body down to him in the water, so he could guide it directly into the deep. I could see the water had reinvigorated his passion, for his body glowed with an unusual heat. "What's in the picnic hamper, Marie? Surely you didn't bring more food! I'm still full from our feast last night!"

"Oh, just some wine and cheese. Some finger food. It seemed fitting since it is a moonlit night, and the company is so delightful!" Daniel grabbed my hand, then my lips. Further conversation was neither necessary nor possible.

Just as he slipped my bikini straps off my shoulders, a spotlight beamed across the water. Daniel raised his head, whispering, "Shit. Bay Patrol. Stay calm. I'll handle this."

"Everything okay over there?" a baritone called across the water. "We got a report of a stranded boat and are checking to see if it was you. Need any help?"

Daniel was trying to unclench his jaw, and it seemed to take forever. As they motored nearer, I raised my head above the gunwales and, obviously adjusting my straps, said crossly, "Honey, what's going on?"

The spotlight swung wildly across the deck and settled on me, obviously in a hurry to smooth my hair and adjust my straps. "Oh, sorry, ma'am. Thought y'all had sent a distress call. Really sorry to have bothered you. Y'all have a good night." The patrol boat quickly sped away.

"Whoa! That was really quick thinking, sweetie! I'm very impressed! Now, where were we. . . ."

—

About an hour before sunrise Daniel dropped me off at my door. He seemed to enjoy more than just a passing fling, particularly since we shared the same peculiar culinary tastes. "Look," he said as he lingered over a long goodnight kiss, "I'm a bit tied up with the club for the next couple of nights. I hate for business to interfere with pleasure, but can I see you in a few days, possibly dinner on Saturday?"

"I wish it didn't have to be so long, Danny, but I can wait. Yes, dinner sounds marvelous. What time? Should I meet you somewhere? What can I bring?"

"No, sweetie, I'll pick you up at nine. There's a delightful little park on the other side of town—dark, secluded, a bit of a lovers' lane, actually. We can have a marvelous time there, I'm sure." He lingered a moment for another longer, deeper kiss, and reluctantly broke it off. "I need to get home soon, before the early rush! I had a delightful evening. Truly! I know it sounds a bit trite and old-fashioned, but I'm really looking forward to seeing you again. Thank you for everything."

"Oh, Danny, thank YOU! I learned a lot about you tonight, and I look forward to getting to know you even better. You're the true epitome of a gentleman, and I've spent a lot of time looking for someone like you. I feel there's a very strong connection between us, and I want to explore it. With you." I casually touched the small love bite on my neck, tracing my fingertips down to my collarbone, where they lingered. *That should hook him.*

—

Once inside, I went straight to the bathroom and felt my neck. Yes. His ardor had broken the skin, and I could feel the marks of his teeth. No matter. I went into the bedroom and pulled a small journal from under the mattress. *Subject is resourceful, intelligent, flexible, and extremely fit for his age. Evidently, a lot of practice and versatility in disposing of bodies. A messy eater but understands how to clean up after himself, leaving no trace. Has difficulty controlling his passion, his greatest vulnerability, which flares quickly. Considering his age, it is either carelessness or overconfidence. Either way, he is a liability. Will need to proceed with caution.*

I replaced the journal, pulled out a Tracfone, texted a quick message, and hit send. I turned off the phone, replaced it with the journal, crawled into bed, and slept like one dead until late afternoon.

———

As far as the neighbors are concerned, I work from home as a graphic designer, doing website design and a bit of marketing. But most of my work is online. Three large monitors and my light-sensitive eyes are the reason the curtains are drawn all the time. I entertain clients in the evenings when necessary, usually downtown. My cover is good; I've used it for years, and it has never been broken.

Slowly and methodically, I have risen in the Family, and I'm now one of their top enforcers. Daniel is the oldest and highest-ranking member of the Family I've been assigned to investigate and, possibly, deal with. The Family is my life—they rescued me from a horrible death years ago, and I owe them everything. I had been brutally and savagely attacked by a band of marauders and was near death when a wandering Yankee found me. He, thankfully, knew what to do, although it felt at the time like death would have been easier. When I was well enough to travel, he took me to the Family for a longer recovery.

I had started out as simply a stray, someone who had been saved. Once

I had learned to control my new and wild appetites, my intelligence, common sense, and loyalty caught the attention of my superiors. They slowly increased my responsibilities over the years, moving me from simply research and information-gathering to surveillance and actual enforcing. I'm good at what I do. I'm well-trained, have excellent control and acting skills, and my track record is impeccable. My star is rising, and Daniel is the key.

—

Promptly at nine, there was a brief tap on the door. I was ready, casually dressed in a dark blue spaghetti-strap dress that flowed around my knees and accentuated my neckline, waist, and dewy complexion. Daniel was even more casual—jeans, high-end sneakers, and a different Rolex. He definitely was taking care of himself. His tan had been carefully reapplied, and he looked like any prosperous, middle-aged businessman.

"Wow, right on time! I'm impressed! And I'm so looking forward to dinner! I'm so hungry I could eat a horse!" I made sure the little southern nuances were there, catching his attention and keeping him off guard.

"Sorry, I hadn't thought of putting Dobbin on the menu tonight, but we can change plans if you want. Or keep our date in Lovers' Lane. Up to you, m'lady!"

"Oh, Daniel," I cooed, "Lovers' Lane sounds right up my alley. And I've been anticipating this for days!"

We arrived at the little park in about 45 minutes. Once we parked, I took in the scenery while Daniel fiddled with something under the hood. This was the highest hill near the city, and the overlook offered a spectacular view looking east over the skyline. This was an ideal spot. No wonder so many couples came up here. The seclusion and privacy, the vista, the beautiful landscape, it was all just perfect for romance. I grabbed the picnic hamper, and we strolled, arm in arm, up the trail.

"C'mere, gorgeous. There's a spot just up here where we can toss the blanket and keep an eye on the path while we wait and get to know each other better. So, really, how long have you been in the city? How come I've never run into you out and about? Tell me all about your background, your family, what you actually do."

We both knew what we were—just two old souls trying to find a way to fit in and not be noticed. Daniel had had a number of occupations, some rather close to the limits of the law, but none so close that he ever got caught. He never stayed in a city for more than 15 years, depending on its size and how easily he could move around. This nightclub was his newest venture, and he loved not only the easy money but the gorgeous young creatures who were attracted to the liquor, the ambiance, and the music. "I'll need to move on within a year or so since it's getting more difficult to hide my age. These kids want young rockers. People that are hip to the latest thing. I'm getting a little old for them, and the struggle between staying young and hip and maintaining a semblance of age in this internet and social media era is driving me crazy. How about you? You've obviously been around a while. You know the ropes, the dodges, the alternate stories. How'd you wind up here, of all places?"

"Yeah," I said, "I know what you're talking about. I've watched things change from jalopies to hot rods to turbos; newspapers to online instant news. Waiting tables, prostitution, secretary, I was even a gun moll for a time. But now, I'm just a simple work-at-home graphic designer with high-paying clients and a clean record. I'm not actually off the grid, just under it. Out of sight and out of mind. No one notices the average ones.

"Before I was changed, I wanted to do something with some responsibility, not just be a wife and mother. That changed real fast when I was about 20, and the final encounter of my short, dead-end life gave me a new purpose, a new direction, a new life. The sky was the limit, and now I'm reaching for it!"

As we talked softly, I realized why Daniel favored this spot. The couples who came up here were usually young and had more difficulty in fending off his advances. He was incredibly wise about human behavior, and he used that to his advantage, lulling these naïve youngsters into a false sense of security. His initial appearance was non-threatening, a hip nightclub owner, car trouble, and an unseen "hot date" who was getting nervous about being stranded on this hillside. Vague promises about getting them into the club, even if they were underage, usually sealed the deal. He had been working this angle for years now and had a great routine set up to dispose of the bodies and the cars. As far as anyone knew, the couples had simply disappeared over the border, off on a new life and fantastic adventures.

Daniel was not aware that the disappearances were now at a tipping point, and the Family was concerned about the pattern becoming more apparent. Anonymity, for the Family, was paramount.

That's where I came in. Daniel was causing problems for the Family, and I was the enforcer who had to do something about it. Our research and surveillance had only gotten us so far. Daniel was good at covering his tracks, but he'd been here too long, and suspicions were being raised. It wouldn't be long before something came out. The Family had to act now before it became a scurry to the underground until things blew over. But this new technology meant we would have to stay underground longer than we'd ever had to, and there were some who wouldn't make it. Better to sacrifice one, if necessary, than many.

Trying to steer the conversation away from me and my "cover," I sweetly whispered, "You know an awful lot about me, Danny, but what about you? Have you always been a nightclub owner?" Men do like to talk about themselves, especially when they have a captive audience. "How long have you been 'special'?"

"I don't mean to brag or sound egotistical, but I'm over 450 years old. I arrived in this country when it was just being explored by the Europeans, and I took a job as an able seaman to escape what was going on in Spain. They thought they could get rid of us by simply burning us. Their so-called heretics, yes. But us, burning just makes us angry. I feasted on a few of those 'superior' clerics before I sailed. And a good thing I did, too. Disappearances of crew on a small ship get noticed quickly.

"I worked mostly below decks and was always able to take the night watches, so the crew pretty much left me alone. Once we landed, I grabbed some clothing and vanished. The native populations were soon scared enough of me that I became legend, mythic, and powerful enough that they willingly gave me sacrifices. I moved from time to time just to avoid overharvesting the population, and I've seen most of this country. Adequate shelter was sometimes difficult, but I carried a heavy blanket, and I made sure to be out of sight when the sun rose.

"The wars were always a good opportunity for me because disabled wounded were everywhere. It was a time of great joy and freedom. I didn't have to stay so hidden, and food was plentiful. No one thought anything of another body to be disposed of—just another victim of a stray arrow, or bullet, or shell. Good times, yes, good times."

"Wow, Daniel! I'd have never thought you were so old and experienced! No wonder all of this—the stalking, the kill, the disposal of evidence—seems so easy for you. Does this modern technology create a problem?"

"Nothing I can't handle. I make sure to never have my picture taken, not that it matters. We can't be photographed! I find that laughable. Even the most modern technology can't catch us! Immortal, unstoppable, irresistible, and always hungry! I was made for this era!" He laughed low in his chest.

"Do you hear that? Is that footsteps, or just a deer?"

"Let me look. Yeah. A luscious couple of kids. They seem so intent on each other, they won't notice me. Back in a few."

Daniel followed them for about 100 yards, and I could hear his voice.

I won't go into the messy details. Suffice it to say that Daniel's smooth patter and "middle-aged man in distress" act was enough for the young man to show his true love just what kind of white knight he could be. And the promise of getting them into the club, even though they were underage, was enough to lure them to the car. Daniel played the role of a nightclub owner fooling around with a client's wife very convincingly. Especially when there was a "distraught" female companion adding to the confusion. When the young man bent over the open hood while I started the Rover, Daniel said, "I just don't know why it won't start." I took care of the girlfriend.

———

Once we'd eaten and rested a bit, we needed to dispose of the bodies. Daniel picked up the male, and I grabbed the girl. She wasn't that heavy and was fairly easy to carry to the edge of the overlook. I had seen earlier that there was a pretty sheer drop to piles of boulders below us. Anything that fell over the edge had a good chance of remaining unseen and undiscovered for a long while. Again, we stripped them of their clothes and personal possessions before watching them tumble down. Insects would take care of what the foxes and other carrion eaters didn't. All that would be left would be bones bleaching in the bright sun.

While I tidied up at the overlook, Dan went back to get our blanket and hamper. When he returned, he reattached the distributor cable and tossed the blanket in the back of the SUV. I dug around in the outside pocket of the hamper, looking for my lipstick. "Daniel, wait a minute, sweetie. I need to go back. I think I left my lipstick back there."

"Fine. I'll call my guy about their car. I won't be long."

Once I was out of his eyesight, I scampered up to where the couple had been. Yes, I found it. The wallet the young man had taken out of his pocket when things began getting hot and heavy with his girlfriend.

I walked back to our car, the wallet clutched in my hand. "Daniel. I need to talk to you. I think we have a problem."

"What, sweetheart? Do you want to linger a little longer? I can get the blanket out of the back."

"You missed something. When we stripped the kids, didn't you notice the boy didn't have a wallet on him? I went back to look for it and found it. Here. Put it in the bag with the other things we need to get rid of."

This was the tipping point. I had to keep Daniel off his guard. "Okay, Marie. That's just a minor detail. C'mere. Kiss and make up? It was just a little mistake. It won't happen again."

I had had my back to him while I fiddled with the hamper on the front seat. "No, Dan, I don't think it will." I struck him with all the force I could muster. The stake I had pulled out of the unused hamper penetrated his chest. He screamed. I pushed the stake in as far as I could. Dan thrashed about; he stumbled, holding on to my arms. He struck out at me and knocked me off the overlook. The last thing I remembered was that I was flying, flying, flying.

—

I had a dreadful headache. Hot. I was hot. Oh, God, it was the sun. Death rode in those beams of light. I crawled as quickly as I could behind a large boulder. Temporary shelter. I could stay here for a bit until my headache eased, but then what? I cautiously opened my eyes.

The bodies of those two kids were just feet away. If I tried to reach them, the sun would incinerate me before I could get six inches. I could only hope for rescue, and the odds were not in my favor.

The heat continued over the course of the next few hours as I crawled further and further under the boulder. Shelter. I needed shelter. And the clouds were no help. I dozed in a fitful stupor. It could have been minutes or hours. I didn't know. But the light had faded, and there was a smell of ozone in the air. The thunderstorm hit quickly, rain pouring from the sky. I scrambled over to the bodies and dragged them back to the boulder. Perhaps they would provide enough cover to protect me from that hated sun.

—

I was surprised to open my eyes, having thought I would never open them again. The bodies were already starting to swell and stink. I looked up at the overlook, wondering how I could ever climb back up that sheer face. The night was cool on my skin, and a welcome relief.

I noticed a small trail off to the left. There was an odor of fox and raccoon about it, but at least it was easy walking. I took off my shoes, amazed they were still on my feet. It would be easier barefoot than in those open-toed heels if I had to climb that hill. The trail led to another branching path, and I chose paths that led upward. I eventually reached a guardrail and crawled over. A few hundred more yards and I reached the pull-over. The Rover was still there. Off toward the edge of the overlook, there was a wet smear of black ash that trickled to a drainage hole in the rock wall. All that remained of Daniel was his wallet, his keys, a ring, and a blackened wooden stake. I tossed the stake out into the night air and climbed into the vehicle.

———

The rest was easy. I drove home with a hamper of jewelry, wallets, clothing, grabbed a quick shower, got into some sensible clothes, and drove the Rover downtown to Daniel's club. I parked in his spot, grabbed the keys out of the ignition, and walked away. There was no evidence in the SUV to link me to him and no evidence up on the hill. I'm good at what I do, albeit not figuring how he would thrash about when I drove that stake into his heart. Thankfully, the thunderstorm had taken care of most of the evidence at the overlook, and the sun ensured there would be no further messages from Daniel.

I walked home as quickly as I could. Jogging had kept me in shape, and I got there quickly. I sent a text to the Family: *Mother, subject has been neutralized. Awaiting further instructions. Will need 24 hours to remove all evidence from this house. Full report will be made upon my return. My regards to Father.* I put the phone back under the mattress with my journal, now complete.

"she has no need to chase.
she sits quietly,
her patience a consummate force..."

Donna Lynn Hope

Before she's Gone Forever

Phil Giunta

It took the entire morning, but police divers found Eun-ji's body in the bay—exactly where I said it would be. I wasn't entirely forthcoming with them, of course. I didn't tell them about the pictures. I simply informed them that Eun-ji had talked about exploring the peaks of Geoje Island to find a good spot for cliff jumping. Fearless and heavily influenced by western culture, Eun-ji was what the Americans call an "adrenaline junkie." Hence the reason she had volunteered for civilian military training in the city of Gimpo last month. That's where we met.

As a photographer for the *Korea Herald,* I had been assigned to shoot the weeklong boot camp. My mandatory two years in the Army had just ended six months prior, so I was still able to keep up with the grueling regimen these college students faced. Nothing extraordinary had occurred during the assignment—other than meeting Eun-ji. Day or night, my camera loved her more than any of the others…

—

The air inside the converted airplane hangar retained the chill of an early spring morning as the first squad prepared for their afternoon run. The enormous arched building had been repurposed as a combination barracks, garage, and storage facility, all for the purposes of operating the training camp organized by a group of retired Marines. Clutching my camera to my chest, I weaved around bodies and equipment, scanning the area for Eun-ji. She'd caught my attention earlier in the day with her flawless performance through the obstacle course. Since then, the trainees had changed from helmets to black berets, making it easier to recognize faces. Finally, I spotted her near the open hangar door, boring through an old truck tire with a power drill.

I took a few shots as she handed off the tool to another trainee and pushed an eye bolt through the hole in the rubber. After securing it with nut and washer, she attached both ends of a chain to the eye with a carabiner and looped a tow strap through the chain. A moment later, the strap was clipped to a harness around Eun-ji's narrow waist and shoulders. Just as they had for the past two mornings, the trainees would run the width of the field while pulling tires tethered to their upper bodies—a standard military exercise.

"Impressive." I took another shot as she drew herself to her full height. "You made quick work of that, just like the obstacle course."

"It's the third time this week I had to rig one of these." She barely glanced at me before returning her attention to her task. "What's your name again?"

"Joon-hyuk."

"Is there a reason you keep following me, Joon-hyuk?"

"You're incred—" My words were smothered by the whine and roar of power drills all around us. Eun-ji tilted her head and twisted her lips into a lopsided smirk until the clamor ceased, allowing me to finish. "You're incredibly photogenic."

She lowered her demure gaze and pretended to adjust her harness. "Well, thank you, but I need to join my squad now ... or didn't you notice the other dozen people around us?" She trudged out of the hangar toward the field of dry sandy scrub across the tarmac.

"Of course, I did. I'm here to photograph as many of you as possible." I waited until both she and her burden were out of the hangar's shadow before taking a few more shots. "Need me to carry that tire for you?"

"I can handle it, funny boy. I like pushing myself. That's why I'm here."

We walked the rest of the way in silence and arrived just as the sergeant ordered everyone to fall in.

"Good luck." I stopped at the edge of the field and raised my camera. "See you later?"

"Maybe."

I took several shots as she lined up with her squad. A minute later, the sergeant fired into the air, and the trainees started off, legs pumping. Some staggered at first, dragging their tires like boat anchors, but not Eun-ji. Despite a slow start, she maintained her footing and bolted toward the trees, tire gouging up a continuous cloud of dust in her wake.

—

I shared dinner with over two dozen inquisitive university students—

entertaining them with stories from my army days so they knew what to expect when their time came—but Eun-ji sat with a group of young women at the opposite end of the hall. I didn't have the chance to chat her up again until after midnight when two bellowing sergeants roused exhausted trainees out of their bunks and back to the field. They were each handed a K2 assault rifle with laser sight and divided into groups of five while the sergeants explained the concept of the drill. Just inside the tree line, targets had been hung. When they flashed a green light, the trainees opened fire. A red light signaled for them to stop.

The first group lined up as ordered, and the sergeants allowed me one minute to take pictures. Fortunately, Eun-ji was in the first group, her face still smudged with green and black camouflage paint from the previous day's exercises.

"You again," she groaned.

"To be fair, I was out here before any of you. I knew this was coming, so I stayed around to get pictures."

"Thanks for the warning."

I lifted my camera to take a close-up, but when I peered through the viewfinder, Eun-ji was gone. She had dropped to one knee, turned her cap backward, and leveled her rifle toward the tree line, its stock braced against her shoulder. I moved beside her and crouched down just as a pair of sergeants approached. I didn't have much time. "Come on. Just one close-up."

Without a word, Eun-ji glanced at me, her expression conveying a trace of annoyance. I snapped the picture and moved away just as one of the sergeants came to a halt behind Eun-ji. Ignoring me, he ordered the trainees to take aim. In the woods, green lights flashed, and rubber bullets flew.

———

I left Gimpo on the last train of the night and returned to my office in Seoul the next morning, where I uploaded the photos to my workstation. As I reviewed each one, cropping and adjusting as necessary, Eun-ji was far from my thoughts—until I found myself staring at that last close-up shot. I'd taken over a dozen photos of Eun-ji in action throughout the day, but there was something different about that one. Perhaps it was the mere stillness of the moment that allowed my lens to capture the slightest hint of anxiety—*or was it fear?*—that had been otherwise concealed by her bravado. Then again, being roused from sleep at midnight by a shrieking whistle and two barking drill sergeants would rattle anyone's nerves.

"Nice shot."

I swiveled my chair to find my smirking editor standing in the doorway.

"Then again, you always did have an eye for the attractive ones," he continued. "I assume you managed to take at least a few shots of the other trainees?"

"Scores of them." I pressed the arrow keys to start scrolling through the Gimpo photos.

"Good. Pick the best dozen or so and send them to me for review. We'll get them on the website by the end of the day. When are you going to the K Museum?"

"They open at ten. I plan to go there first, get shots of the new Jega Pop Culture exhibit, then send you the best of those and Gimpo."

With a nod, he continued down the corridor.

After counting to seven, I rolled my chair to the door and leaned out just as he stepped into his office. *Like clockwork.*

I leapt to my feet, shoved my chair under my desk, and checked the bus schedule online. From Yonhap Station, it was 43 minutes to the K Museum of

Contemporary Art. Today, though, it would take me over two hours via train and bus—by way of Gimpo. Knowing my editor, he wouldn't notice my extended absence as long as I submitted my work on time.

But first, I had to see Eun-ji again before she was gone forever.

———

It was the final day of civilian boot camp, and fortunately, the guards at the gate were the same ones from the day before. They recognized me immediately and, after I passed a security check, allowed me back onto the grounds under the pretense that I'd misplaced an expensive zoom lens somewhere on the property.

After thanking them, I rushed to the women's barracks and found three of the trainees packing their bags. I knocked on the open door. "Excuse me. I'm sorry to intrude, but can you tell me where I might find Eun-ji?"

The woman closest to me zipped her bag and slung it over her shoulder. "You just missed her. She left a few minutes ago. You're the photographer that was here yesterday."

"Yes."

"You looking for a date with her?"

At that, the other two laughed.

"Did she say where she was going?"

"Oh, *babo* is smitten," another woman said. "Everyone noticed how you were hanging around her."

"I don't know where she lives"—the first woman brushed past me—"but she mentioned a hiking trip to Geoje Island in a week or two. She wanted to go cliff jumping later in the spring. Maybe you can find her on Kakao. Good luck, lover boy."

—

Back in the office later that afternoon, I sent all of the pictures to my editor, then logged into Kakao, the social media site, and found Eun-ji after a few minutes. I sent her a message. When days passed with no response, I sent another. That, too, went unanswered. I gave up for fear of making a nuisance of myself.

At home a few weeks later, I decided to review all the shots I'd taken over the past several assignments. I'd saved copies of them to my laptop, and it was time to clean them out since I had backed them up to my cloud storage.

When I opened the close-up of Eun-ji, taken that night in the field, I realized instantly that something had changed. Her lips were parted slightly as if she'd been speaking when I took the shot—but that wasn't how I remembered it. I logged into my cloud storage and opened the photo from there. As expected, Eun-ji's mouth was closed. Confused, I saved the second image with a different filename then fell asleep staring at both photos on my screen.

—

I woke up to complete darkness just after three in the morning. It took me a moment to remember that I was still sitting in my living room. With a yawn, I reached over and turned on the table lamp, nearly knocking my laptop to the floor in the process. I caught it before it slid off my lap and tapped the space bar to wake the screen. *Were the two different shots of Eun-ji merely a dream?* After logging back in, I found myself staring at Eun-ji once more—and this time, not only was her brow furrowed but her mouth wide open as if silently shouting at me.

"What the hell is going on here?" I tore my gaze away from the screen, anticipating a response from someone lurking in the shadows. *This has to be a joke.* Yet, the image didn't appear to be Photoshopped. I suddenly felt uncomfortable sitting in the dark. I leaped from my seat and turned on the other floor lamp and the television. Finally, I returned to my laptop and saved this third image.

After a quick shower and breakfast, I resolved to determine what was happening with these photos of Eun-ji. What had been one photo was now three. I logged back on to my laptop and immediately regretted it. Eun-ji's expression had changed from anger to distress. Her lips were now pursed, and her eyes glistened with fear. By the time I started breathing again, I reached out with a trembling hand and clicked the Save button yet again.

I distracted myself with an online game until dawn. Part of me wanted to crawl into bed, but I had to figure out where these pictures were coming from. It occurred to me then to disable my Wi-Fi connection in case someone was remotely connected and copying these images to my laptop. Fleetingly, I wondered if Eun-ji herself had hacked me and was playing a prank. I couldn't wait around to find out. I had to catch the train to work.

—

After pressing the button for the elevator, I leaned against the wall for a catnap—which lasted all of eight seconds before the chime forced my reluctant eyes open. I pushed away from the wall just as the doors parted to reveal my neighbor, Seul-ki, bundled up as if she'd just returned from an expedition to the Arctic Circle. Although it was a time of year that brought mild afternoons, early morning hours were often still frigid, especially to a petite little kitten like Seul-ki. She lowered the scarf from her face and flashed a smile that made my eyes glad the rest of me had been too exhausted to take the stairs. Seul-ki was around the same age as Eun-ji and even more photogenic. In Seul-ki's case, though, my camera wasn't the only one who loved her.

Stepping out of the elevator, she pulled off her gloves and signed a greeting. "Hi, Joon-hyuk. You look exhausted. Rough night?"

Seul-ki had been born deaf but was adept at reading lips. Despite that, I had asked her to start teaching me sign language last week. Any excuse to spend more time with her. I replied as well as my limited vocabulary allowed but spoke slowly at the same time. "Bizarre night. I think my computer's haunted, or maybe my camera, or maybe it's me..."

"I don't understand." Seul-ki motioned.

"It would take too long to explain."

The elevator doors began to close. I stepped over the threshold and held them open as Seul-ki nodded toward her apartment at the end of the hall. "How about dinner at my place tonight? You can tell me all about it."

"I'd love it! See you then."

I resumed my catnap on the way down.

—

I knew better than to contact Gimpo. The military would never release any personal information. Instead, I decided to post my original close-up of Eun-ji on Kakao in the hope that someone could put me in touch with her. A few people responded but claimed that they had not seen or spoken to Eun-ji in weeks.

I heard the approaching footsteps even before the knock on my office door. I minimized the image of Eun-ji just as my editor barged into my office. "You look like hell. Are you sick?"

"Didn't sleep well."

"You in shape to go out?"

"I was in shape to come in."

"Funny. I know you're covering the railway expansion in a few hours. When you're done there, I need you to go with Hyun-woo and get some shots of the press conference for the new Hanwha corporate office opening in Incheon."

"No problem."

I waited until he was out of sight, counted to seven again, and heard his office door close before bringing up Eun-ji's picture. I wasn't surprised to see that her expression had changed yet again, but it was no less unsettling. Her wide eyes conveyed far more desperation than in any of the previous images. It was as if she were pleading for help with… what? I still had no clue, so I saved this one with a new filename in the same folder with the others. I now had seven new photos of Eun-ji that I'd never shot, each one a variation of my original. By now, I was convinced that this was no prank. I took time to fully examine each image but detected no evidence of fabrication.

I've never believed in the supernatural, but I couldn't help worrying that something had happened to Eun-ji and that she was reaching out to me through these pictures. I checked the *Korea Herald* and *Yonhap News* websites for breaking reports of a missing woman, a fatal accident, or even a murder. The most dramatic stories involved two arrests for rape and one for child endangerment. Neither mentioned anyone named Eun-ji.

Unfortunately, I didn't have time to investigate further. I locked my computer and packed my camera, but I couldn't get her out of my mind. Even as I focused on the day's assignments, I was anxious to see the next picture of Eun-ji—and to solve this disturbing mystery.

—

After dinner at Seul-ki's apartment later that night, she asked me to explain what I'd babbled about that morning at the elevator.

I hesitated, concerned that she might think I was crazy, but I was emboldened by the fact that I had photos to prove my bizarre experiences. I opened my laptop, logged into my cloud account, and showed her the original photo I had taken of Eun-ji at Gimpo.

Seul-ki curled her mouth into a lopsided smirk. "You always find the pretty ones, don't you?"

I looked over at her to ensure that she could read my lips. "Why do you think I like spending time with you?"

At that, she blushed. "I thought it was just for the food."

"That's a bonus."

Still smirking, Seul-ki averted her gaze and nodded at the laptop. "So, what's her story?"

"That's what I'm trying to figure out. This was the only close-up I took of her." I logged out of my cloud account and opened the folder on my hard drive. "See all of these files? They're photos of Eun-ji that I never took. Like this one." I opened the first variation that I had saved early that morning. "It looks similar to the original, but notice her lips are slightly parted, and her eyes seem more intense. Every time I opened this folder today, new close-ups appeared out of nowhere, each one different. As of this morning, I had seven alternate images. Look…"

I closed the picture of Eun-ji—only to find that six new files had been created in the last ten seconds! Seul-ki noticed them, too. We exchanged glances before I checked my network connection. It was offline, of course. I didn't have the password to Seul-ki's Wi-Fi—which meant no one could have downloaded these files to my laptop.

"Are you going to open them?" Seul-ki asked.

My trembling hand hovered over the trackpad. "I never had more than one show up at a time."

I held my breath until all six images were lined up across my screen. I forced myself to speak slowly so that Seul-ki could read my lips. "Look at her face. It's as if she's becoming more frightened with each one."

Seul-ki leaned forward. "She is!" Her hands were almost a blur. Fortunately, she spoke as quickly as she signed. "I didn't recognize her at first with the camouflage face paint, but that's the woman that went missing yesterday."

"*What?*"

"You're in the news business. You didn't hear about it?"

"I checked online as soon as I got to the office. I didn't see anything about her."

"The story just broke. I read it on my phone. She was hiking on Geoje Island yesterday and was separated from her friends. When they couldn't find her, they called the police. She's still missing." Seul-ki stared at the screen. "Wait. Can you tile all thirteen images in consecutive order?"

"Sure, but I'll need to do it in two rows."

A minute later, I stared at the photos as Seul-ki pointed to each one in turn, her eyes welling up. "Read her lips. She's telling us where she is. *I'm drifting in the bay north of Geoje.* Joon-hyuk, this woman is dead. What's worse, she died alone. Her soul is *kaekkwi*, a wandering ghost. She's been trying to communicate with you through these pictures."

I dropped back in my chair, struggling to accept what I had feared was true. Reading Eun-ji's lips hadn't even occurred to me. *Did she lose her footing at the precipice of a cliff and plunge into the bay? Did she die instantly, or did she drown?*

A tap on my shoulder forced my gaze away from the imploring eyes of Eun-ji to the tear-streaked face of Seul-ki. She moved her hands slowly this time but still spoke aloud for emphasis. "We need to call the police. Have them search the waters north of Geoje before the tide washes her body out to the strait. Before she's gone forever."

—

At work two days later, I caught up with the reporter covering the story and learned that Eun-ji's service was being held that morning at a *Jang rae sik jang*, a funeral home, in Daejeon. Her funeral would last the standard three days. Afterward, she would be cremated.

I considered attending, but I barely knew her, and I didn't want to risk dishonoring her memory or upsetting her family with outlandish tales of spectral photographs. They might not have believed me anyway. Many people in my generation and younger put little stock in such legends as the kaekkvi. I didn't either, until this. I could only hope that now, surrounded by her family, Eun-ji's soul had found peace.

Reluctantly, I opened the folder on my workstation where I had saved every variation of Eun-ji's close-ups, but where there had been thirteen, there were now only five. I checked the time stamp on the files. They had been created two nights ago, approximately an hour after her body was recovered.

The file names each ended in a number, so I opened them in sequential order until they were tiled across my monitor. Eun-ji's soft features were unblemished by camouflage paint and her hair, no longer gathered beneath a cap, cascaded down her shoulders. Though her expression was placid, I didn't need a camera lens to reveal the obvious sorrow in her eyes, nor did I need Seul-ki's lip-reading skills to understand Eun-ji's final message.

Gomabseubnida.

Thank you.

Porch Ghost

as recounted by Dianne Pearce[*]

This story was told to me by my old friend Dutton Cordray, who worked at his corner market in Pepperbox. I used to stop by there for a coffee on my drive to work in the morning, off the main roads to miss the chicken trucks, and got friendly with Mista-Dray, as everyone called him. Little by little, as the store got emptier and emptier and people went to the Royal Farms, Mr. Dray and I got talking to each other longer and longer, and when he found out that I liked to both write and read ghost stories, he told me about the porch ghost. How he came to know about it, not having been there at the time, I can't imagine, and couldn't bring myself to be rude enough to ask. But, since Mr. Dray passed last year, at the ripe old age of 93, and the store in Pepperbox stands sadly empty, I did start asking around. As far as I can tell, folks from Pepperbox to Stockley to Northwest Hundred know the story and speak of it as

---

[*]From the forthcoming Gravelight collection, *Fair Warnings: Being a Forthright and Perfidious Compendium of the Legends and Folklore of Sussex County and Parts Adjacent.*

fact. The porch in question once resided just to the west of Stockley, right about where Stockley Road hit into Stockley Branch, some say, but there's a development of fine stick-built houses there now. Others I've spoken with say that, even after what happened, the family had a lot of weight in the county, and the Bethesda United Methodist Church appeared on the spot, as if to cover up the whole thing with God, almost before the fire went cold.

But, I'm getting ahead of my story.

It starts, as many ghost stories do, with a woman crying. The ghost started visiting Coralee after her son, Boone, was jailed for rape and awaiting trial. Macon, Husband to Coralee and Daddy to Boone, came from one of the richest families in Sussex and had, in his youth, won the heart of Coralee, the Teen Miss Blades of 1947, and prom queen at the next high school over from his. Though it was often said that Macon had fathered children all over Sussex and Wicomico counties, Coralee was not built for childbearing, and Boone was her only, and much revered, son. The signature had barely dried on Boone's high school diploma when he was jailed for rape after being accused by a fellow student, Brisa DeLeon. Boone went into the local lockup, unable to get bail because of the severity of the attack on DeLeon and scuttlebutt in the community that this may not have been the first time Boone had acted with violence against a female. Macon went out nightly, "Trying to figure out how to goddamn save Boone from a long stint inside!" he said. Coralee, left behind, sat on her porch, worried and all alone, weeping quietly and sipping on a warm Coca-Cola through a striped paper straw, 'til the night the ghost walked out of the cornfield, up onto the porch, and sat plumb in the other rocker as like she'd always been there.

And you may rightly wonder about a woman, such as Coralee, who, when a ghost come up out of the cornfield and sat next to her on her porch, didn't run screaming into the house or to the deep blue Bel Air that was only used for church or when Coralee went to get her hair done. But really, it was not hard to understand. Coralee was so deep in her thoughts about poor Boone that she certainly didn't notice the ghost immediately. And the ghost was just a collection of fog trapped in a body-shaped cloud. Everyone thought Coralee had a pretty face and not too much to speak of inside the head behind the face, but she was not so dumb as to be afraid of a body-shaped cloud. The ghost was comforting; sat quietly as Coralee talked. And Coralee was lonely for listening; it was good just to have someone there to hear her. It never even occurred to Coralee that this was a ghost, a ghost sitting plumb in the other rocker, Macon's rocker. No, she was just glad of the ear, spectral as it may have been. The ghost was mannered, respectful, of Macon's rocker and Coralee, never interrupted, stayed on the porch as long as Coralee did, and seemed to understand.

"He's so handsome." Coralee said this, or something similar, each night, and the cloud of ghost seemed to nod in agreement. "It's not fair. Young people with their lives ahead of them should not be made to suffer." The ghost always seemed to puff up a bit with glow when Coralee said this, and Coralee felt that the ghost understood. Each night the conversation went the same way. Coralee would settle herself into the rocker after Macon left out. The night would get later, the Coca-Cola would grow warm, and Coralee's worry would increase until the tears came, and the ghost appeared between the tall cornstalks that went right up to the kitchen side of the house and walked out onto the gravel and up the wooden steps to the porch of the fine Amish stick-built home. The long hours would pass more quickly, and, deep into the early morning, Macon still not home, Coralee would finally rise and incline her head to the ghost in a goodnight, go inside, and sleep like a baby. The ghost never followed, just rose up from the rocker at the nod of Coralee's head and turned and walked, tall and straight as a fully gossamer body can be, back into the corn on the kitchen side of the house.

Things weren't going so easy for Boone. This was distressing to both Macon and Coralee. Macon was often in hushed calls on the phone, and if Coralee would come upon him, he would swipe at her to get away and retreat quickly onto the back staircase, halfway up, halfway down, cord stretched 'til the curls in it were buckled in the opposite direction, to a place where Coralee could not find a way to listen in. If Coralee asked him directly for any information on the case or even how Boone was doing in the jail, why, Macon would swear at her as if she was the dumbest post he'd ever come upon and tell her that these kinds of things were things for men to work on and that Boone didn't need his momma coming down to the jail like he was a baby. Never mind that he was a baby—her baby; she was simply not invited into the details of his predicament, nor was her help wanted in finding a solution.

At least Coralee had her ghost. Macon didn't know about her. Coralee tried and tried to be nosy enough to wait up for Macon to come home from his nights out so she could get some idea of who he was with, what he was up to, but sitting there with the ghost always relaxed her so much she found herself unable to wait up. So Macon never met the ghost.

And the weeks went on, with Coralee talking more and more to her spectral visitor, the only thing that had ever hung on Coralee's every word since she'd said, "I do" to Macon. It's was just so nice to say everything and not be told to hush or stop saying stupid woman things. Each night Coralee got a little more out, a little more mother's love, a little more fear, and a little more anger at the situation her poor boy was in, until the night she said to the understanding ghost, "And you know how vain and mean girls can be. Why, there was a spoilt girl said something about Macon when we was dating, trying to be worth something more than she was, Macon being the special man he is." Coralee sneered these words, and the ghost glowed and rounded out about the middle when she did. Coralee noticed the glow. She felt righteous. "Oh yes, she thought she was special," she said loudly, "but her family knew her worth better, and she just went away. She was gone. They took her away from here, and everyone stopped saying things about my Macon, and everything was like it was supposed to be. It's how come we's married now, and got the wonderful son we got. This girl should too. Stop bothering my dear son, just go away with herself and her jealousy."

The ghost puffed and glowed, big as a moon on the porch, and somehow, after all these nights, this night had managed to get late… enough.

Macon had returned home and saw Coralee on the porch with a girl he thought he'd never see again. Almost before Coralee even realized he was back, Macon grabbed her out of the rocker, dragged her inside, and threw her down, hard and mean like she was nothing to him. And when Coralee hit the floor, she knew she was nothing to him, and the past she had ignored came back into her mind with a bright glowing light, all the rumors about "Pretty girl gone missing," and Coralee knew her porch guest finally, saw how Macon had raped her, and when the girl spoke out, he and his daddy had kidnapped her, choked her, added on the porch for the house right over top of her. Now he was gonna put Boone's girl there—that was his plan!

Just as Macon's hand was swinging down to smack Coralee across her stupid face, the kettle on the stovetop wailed. Macon's head jerked around as the ghost came through the door, a newspaper in her hand with her own face on the front page, the very newsprint blazing with fire. Macon screamed, grabbed his gun from its holster, and shot and shot and shot until he was sure the ghost was dead, but it was Coralee who was dead, and the tea kettle shrieked as the blazing house went up like a tarpaper shack and took Macon right away to hell.

Well, as Mr. Dray told it, the fire department got there first, and though they were certainly too late to save the house, they did pull out Coralee's body before it burned much and saw it was shot full of holes right through the heart. Macon's body was sizzled to a crisp. They couldn't even touch it until the house finally stopped burning. When they did carry him out, they could see he had a scream frozen into the charred bones of his mouth. The chief said he couldn't sleep for a good month afterward without seeing it. The police came soon after the fire, with Bill Barrett and one of his hound dogs, to sniff for accelerant, but the dog went first to the trunk of Macon's Barracuda, where they found a bound and gagged Brisa DeLeon in a large potato sack, out cold, but still alive. Then, when the whole area cooled down two days later, Bill came back with his dog and found the grave, dug deep, under where the porch used to be. And on the ground there, as if it had been placed there brand new that morning, was one perfect and untouched porch rocker, moving a little in the breeze. And some even say that rocker ended up in the parsonage of the United Methodist Church, but only the current pastor knows for sure.

Party Guests

BERNIE BROWN hails from Raleigh, NC. Her debut novel, *I Never Told You*, was published in 2019 and was a finalist in the First Novel category of the Next Generation Indie Book Awards. Bernie has published nearly fifty short stories and essays, is a Pushcart Prize nominee, a writer in residence at the Weymouth Center for the Arts, and a member of Women's Fiction Writers Association and the Author's Guild. Sewing, reading, playing the harmonica, and British television occupy her time when she isn't writing.

More at berniebrownwriter.com

KIM DECICCO is the 2020 Delaware Division of the Arts Fellow in Emerging Fiction. Her short stories have appeared in the *Beach Dreams* anthology and the Rehoboth Beach Writers Guild's group project, *The Objects of Our Lives*—which can be found on their website (fourth installment). Kim lives in southern Delaware, where she divides her time between writing and peddling antiques.

DAVID W. DUTTON (1947–2021) was an author and residential designer who was born and raised in Milton, DE. He wrote three novels as well as numerous short stories and plays. His musical comedy, *oh! Maggie*, created in collaboration with Martin Dusbiber, was produced by the Possum Point Players and the Lake Forest Drama Club. He also wrote the one-act play, *Why the Chicken Crossed the Road*, commissioned and produced by the Delmarva Chicken Festival. In 1997, Dutton was awarded a fellowship as an established writer by the Delaware Arts Council. In 1998, he received a first-place award for his creative nonfiction by the Delaware Literary Connection. His piece, "Who is Nahnu Dugeye?" was subsequently published in the literary anthology, *Terrains*. Dutton's work has appeared in anthologies such as *Suspicious Activity, Solstice, Halloween Party 2019, Equinox*, and *Aurora*. Dutton's *One of the Madding Crowd* was published by Devil's Party Press in 2018 and was awarded best original novel by the Delaware Press Association the following year.

ROBERT FLEMING resides in Lewes, DE. He retired from writing television comedy and game shows to write literary works. Robert's twists bring the reader to the limit to find truth. Robert performed beat-poetry in May 2021 at They-Call-Me-Mitch, an online reading series in San Francisco, CA. In April, his play, *The 8th Wonder,* had a casted reading at the Playwright's Collective. Robert co-hosts a local artist share at the Lewes, DE, library. He is a repeat contributor to Local Gems Press, Radical Fairy Diary, Devil's Party Press, Failed-Haiku, Rehoboth Beach Writer's Guild, Spilled-Ink Virginia, and Camp Rehoboth art show. In June 2021, his writing appeared in the first issue of *The Purposeful Mayonnaise* and the Writer's Journey Blog. His upcoming writing is scheduled to appear in *Ethel Zine* and *Failbetter.*

R. DAVID FULCHER is an author of horror, science fiction, fantasy, and poetry. Major literary influences include H.P. Lovecraft, Dean Koontz, Edgar Allen Poe, Fritz Lieber, and Stephen King. Fulcher's first novel, a historical drama set in World War II, *Trains to Nowhere*, and his second novel, a collection of fantasy and science fiction short stories, *Blood Spiders and Dark Moon*, are both available from authorhouse.com and Amazon. Fulcher's work has appeared in numerous small press publications, including *Lovecraft's Mystery Magazine, Black Satellite, The Martian Wave, Burning Sky, Shadowlands, Twilight Showcase, Heliocentric Net, Gateways, Weird Times, Freaky Frights,* and the anthologies *Dimensions* and *Silken Ropes.* Fulcher's work can also be found in the DPP collection *Halloween Party 2019*, the Gravelight Press Collection *Exhumed: Thirteen Tales too Terrifying to Stay Dead*, available at Amazon. A passion for the written word has also inspired Fulcher to edit and publish the literary magazine, *Samsara* (samsaramagazine.net), which has showcased writers and poets for over a decade. Fulcher resides in Ashburn, VA, with his wife Lisa and their rambunctious cats.

More at rdavidfulcher.com

PHIL GIUNTA enjoys crafting powerful fiction that changes lives and inspires readers. His novels include the paranormal mysteries *Testing the Prisoner*, *By Your Side*, and *Like Mother, Like Daughters*. His short stories appear in such anthologies as *Love on the Edge*, *Scary Stuff*, *A Plague of Shadows*, *Beach Nights, Beach Pulp*, and the *Middle of Eternity* speculative fiction series, which he created and edited for Firebringer Press.

As a member of the Greater Lehigh Valley Writers Group, Phil also penned stories and essays for *Write Here, Write Now; The Write Connections; Rewriting the Past;* and *Writes of Passage*, four of the group's biennial anthologies.

Phil is currently working on the second draft of a science fiction novel while plotting his triumphant escape from the pressures of corporate America, where he has been imprisoned for over twenty-five years.

More at philgiunta.com

MORGAN GOLLADAY has been intrigued with words all her life. Her poetry reflects this, and she uses illusion and allusion in her writing. Much of her work focuses on her native Shenandoah Valley, as well as coastal Delaware.

Golladay has worked with nonprofits as a volunteer and staff member, been a librarian, a blood donor recruiter, and a customer service and purchasing agent for a residential water-well wholesaler. Her watercolor and acrylic-collage paintings have won awards, and she is currently President of the Mispillion Art League in Milford, DE, where she currently lives. An emerging poet, her work has been published in the *Broadkill Review*.

JAMES GOODRIDGE was born and raised in the Bronx and now resides in the Yorkville section of Manhattan. He began writing speculative fiction in 2009. After ten years as a visual artist representative and paralegal, James decided in 2013 to make a better commitment to writing. He is currently at work on a series of short stories in the occult detective genre featuring Madison Cavendish and Seneca Sue—living vampire and werewolf occult detectives. You can find these characters in the horror anthologies *Halloween Party 2019* and *Exhumed* (2020). James has also written a series of *Twilight Zone*-style short stories entitled *The Artwork (I to V)*. He's contributed to numerous anthologies including volumes 1 and 2 of *Scierogenous: An Anthology of Erotic Science Fiction and Fantasy* (2017, 2018), *Sweet, Sexy and Special Dark: Blerdrotica Book 1* (2020), and *Funny as a Heart Attack* (2021). James is a member of the Black Science Fiction Society and runs the Facebook group Who Gives You the Write. More at amazon.com/James-Goodridge/e/B01NH0VN36

JEFFREY D. KEETEN was born on a farm among the flatlands and the endless horizons of North Central Kansas. He's chased and been chased by tornadoes. He's survived dust storms, droughts, and blizzards. He's been stomped by bulls, kicked by horses, and nearly struck by lightning. He left the farm to earn a degree in English Literature from the University of Arizona. While in Tucson, he worked in a bookstore to pay his tuition, which morphed into a ten-year odyssey of managing stores in Arizona and California. He became part owner of a regional, weekly farm publication in Dodge City, and every Friday, as the paper rolled off the presses, he frequently got high on the smell of hot soy ink and the vanilla scent of crisp, new paper. He also owned real estate and rentals but has downshifted away from those endeavors to focus on what he deems most important. Keeten is, first and foremost, a reader. A writer of book reviews. A collector of books. He dabbles with writing fiction. Jeffrey's favorite book is whatever book he's currently reading. He watches the sky with his wife and their Scottish Terrier.

More at jeffreykeeten.com

NANCY NORTH WALKER is a short fiction writer whose stories have appeared in mid-Atlantic anthologies and collections. Her first flash fiction story, "The Confidante," appeared in the summer 2021 issue of *Instant Noodles,* an online literary magazine published by Devil's Party Press. Nancy is currently working on a provocative short story collection about unexpected ways advanced technologies will change our lives in this century, as well as our constructs of what it means to be human. Prior to becoming a creative writer, Nancy spent nearly 40 years as a business communications executive. She was a senior vice president in the Chicago and New York offices of a global public relations firm and later served as vice president of global pharmaceutical communications at a large healthcare company.

More at nancynorthwalker.com

FAYE PEROZICH has been writing for over 30 years, with most of her published work in comics and graphic novels. She first became known for her graphic novel adaptation of Anne Rice's *The Vampire Lestat* in 1989; she would go on to adapt four more of Rice's novels, as well as adapting the works of such authors as Harlan Ellison and Piers Anthony. Her own stories have appeared in dozens of anthologies, including *Angry Shadows* and *Clive Barker's Hellraiser*; she also wrote issues of *Magnus: Robot Fighter*, *Shadowman*, and her own vampire series, *Bloodchilde*. Faye paused her writing career to promote her partner's artwork; "Unwell" is her first published work in ten years. She is currently writing a book of short horror stories.

DIANNE PEARCE has the soul of an entrepreneur, the mind of an anarchist, and the body of an office worker. She used to have the hair of the dog that bit her, but local law enforcement took that away as evidence. She has a lifelong history of helping others, and there is always a meal and a comfortable seat at her house for a friend. She is currently working on finishing her damn novels, in addition to helping bring other's work to print through Devil's Party Press and its imprints.

More at dpearcewrites.com

J.C. RAYE's stories have appeared in anthologies by Scary Dairy Press, Books & Boos, Franklin/Kerr, C. M. Muller, HellBound Books, and Death's Head Press. Other publications are on the way with Belanger Books, Rooster Republic, and Jolly Horror. For 18 years, she's been a professor at a small community college, teaching the most feared course on the planet: public speaking. Witnessing grown people weep, beg, scream, freak out, and collapse is just another delightful day on the job for Raye, and seats in her classes sell quicker than tickets to a Rolling Stones concert. She also loves goats of any kind, even the ones that faint.

RUSSELL REECE's poems, stories, and essays have appeared in a variety of journals and anthologies, including *Blueline*, *The 3288 Review*, *Memoir*

Journal, Crimespree Magazine, Edify Fiction, Under the Gum Tree, The Broadkill Review, and others. Reece has received fellowships in literature from the Delaware Division of the Arts and the Virginia Center for the Creative Arts. His stories and poetry have received Pushcart and Best of the Net nominations, and awards from the Delaware Press Association and the Faulkner-Wisdom competition. He won the Pat Herold Nielsen Poetry Prize in Chester River Art's 2019 Art of Stewardship contest. Russ lives in rural Sussex County near Bethel, DE, on the beautiful Broad Creek.

More at russellreece.com

DAVID YURKOVICH is a writer, illustrator, and graphic designer. In addition to numerous short stories, he's also authored two prose novels, *Banana Seat Summer* and *Glass Onion,* as well as various graphic novels including *Less Than Heroes, The S.H.o.P., Death by Chocolate: Redux, Altercations, The Broccoli Agenda,* and *Nocturne.* Along with Dianne Pearce, he works to bring manuscripts by unique literary voices to publication through Devil's Party Press and its imprints—Hawkshaw, Out-of-This-World, and Gravelight.

More at yurkoverse.com

"Everything has to come to an end, sometime."

L. Frank Baum

see you at our '23 Gala.

gravelightpress.com

Made in the USA
Middletown, DE
26 September 2021

48350088R00133